Can You See Me?

a novella by

M. R. Williamson

Can You See Me?
by M. R. Williamson

All rights reserved. No part of this book may be reproduced or transmitted in any form or by any means, electronic or mechanical, including photocopying or recording or by any information storage and retrieval systems, without expressed written consent of the author and/or artists.

Can You See Me? is a work of fiction. Names, characters, places, and incidents are products of the author's imagination. Any resemblance to actual events or persons, living or dead, is entirely coincidental.

Story copyright owned by Marvin Williamson
Cover illustration by Sandy DeLuca
Cover design by Laura Givens

First Printing, August 2017
Second Printing, January 2024

Hiraeth Publishing
P.O. Box 1248
Tularosa, NM 88352
e-mail: hiraethsubs@yahoo.com

Visit www.hiraethsffh.com for online science fiction, fantasy, horror, scifaiku, and more. Stop by our online Shop there for novels, magazines, anthologies, and collections. **Support the small, independent press...and your First Amendment rights.**

Also by M. R. Williamson

The Pragamore Chronicles
Curse of the Monkey's Paw
The Angel of Holloway
The Stone Collector
The Moleskin Cap
I, Gnome
Horned Jack
Horned Jack: Nephilim
Horned Jack: Never Say Never
Horned Jack: Pound of Flesh
Mysterious Rider
Snow Mountain Apparition
The Green Lady
Bridges into the Imagination
Bridges into the Imagination 2
Bridges into the Imagination 3

Can You See Me?

Part 1
The Newcomers

Heather Elmore spotted the old home, one hundred yards before they actually got to it. Framed by two, huge weeping willows, it sported a fresh coat of white paint, a forest green roof, and brand new white shudders. Standing proudly, and facing south, it had a gray-green barn on a gentle slope just northeast of it. She slowed, trying to find the words that would convince her children that this was their new home.

"Ohhh wow!" Anna, the oldest, leaned closer to the dash, looking at the old house now coming into view. "Look at that front porch." She hooked her long, blond hair over her left ear. "One more swing and it would be great." But the seventeen-year-old remained strangely quiet as Heather pulled their 1959 white Impala into the drive.

Hailey, the youngest daughter, turned to follow the huge willows as they went past. The wind through the open window played with her long, brown hair as the Impala slowed to a stop. "They're beautiful aren't they? They look as old as grandpa."

"Is this it?" Hunter, the youngest sibling in the clan, quickly sat up in the back seat. The eight-year-old stared at the old barn intently. "I'll bet there's all kinds of things living in there. It looks like it's older than our last school."

"Forget that, young man." Heather glanced back at him. "I don't want you in there until Birmingham checks everything out. There's no telling what's in there. It's been vacant for years."

Hunter laughed, flopping back in his seat. Anna and Hailey sat quietly with a subdued smile. They knew full well that Birmingham wouldn't want to set foot in a place like that. The old colored fellow was a great handyman, and his wife, Mrs. Emily, had been with them so long they seemed like family. But they well knew Birmingham Jones' limitations. Eight-legged and no-legged critters, monsters, and ghosts were certainly not his strong points.

"Uhhh . . ." Hailey eyed the old house with a jaundiced shade. "Are we getting out?"

Heather opened the door, barely glancing at her daughter as they got out. "I don't want to connect with any negative expressions this early, young lady," she warned. "Let's take a closer look."

"You bet." Hunter popped open the door and hopped out, eyeing the barn as he did so.

"Ohhh no." Heather tightened the band on her blond ponytail as she looked straight at her son. "We're not going exploring just yet. Your father and the van will be here any minute young man. It's well before noon. Everybody will have to help in setting this place up. You three will start on your rooms first. Mrs. Emily and Birmingham have already provided us with a jump on the cleaning, but the house is as far as they have gone. Absolutely no wandering around out here."

♎   ♎   ♎

Susan Christopher stood gazing out of her upstairs bedroom window. Across the roof of the porch, she could see the big white Chevrolet and those around it.

So that's why the colored couple were cleaning this place so hard. Are we to have guests again?"

The petite, hazel-eyed eight-year-old brushed her long, blond hair back behind her ears and eased closer to the window. Although several drove up and down the main road, very few pulled into the drive, especially after dark. Up and down the gravel road she looked, but there was still not a sign of her father's big, red, Chrysler Newport. She knew it was almost time for him and her mom and she missed their hugs and kisses. But as she watched, a huge, yellow van pulled into the drive followed by a silver, Ford pickup.

I couldn't have missed Dad's Chrysler." She checked the road again. *"We can't have guests like this if he isn't here.*

She wheeled and raced from her bedroom only to pause at the head of the stairway.

Maybe they're just friends and Mom and Dad will be here any minute.

She eased down the stairway with her eyes glued to the stained glass, double doors in the living room. There was still no one on the front porch. Stopping near the bottom, she noticed someone's shape through the windows. Even though the image was distorted by the glass, she could tell it was a colored person.

A metallic rattle came from the lock. It was the type of sound one would make while trying the door knob.

"Intruders!" She jumped the remaining steps and ran for the coat closet left of the front door. Slowing as she passed the doors oval windows, she could see there were now more than one on the porch, and a small silver pickup had pulled up behind the Impala. On to the closet she raced.

♎ ♎ ♎

Birmingham froze with his hand on the door knob. Stepping around the two boxes he had sat down in front of him, he slowly moved his head from side to side in search of a clearer pane. Short, a bit portly, and almost bald, he straightened up, rubbing his head.

"Birmingham!" A tall and thin white man fidgeted right behind him, struggling with two large boxes. "Won't the key fit? These things are heavy you know."

"Didn't use the key. Thought I had left it open."

"Well try the key," grumbled the white man.

Birmingham hesitated. Glancing back, he added, "Thought I saw someone in the house." His voice almost a whisper. "Not supposed to be anyone here, Ralph."

"Well, try the key this time. These boxes are heavy."

♎   ♎   ♎

Visitors? Susan eased the door of the coat closet open just enough to see the foyer.

But as she did, another sound came and it wasn't from a doorknob.

"They've got a key! How can that be?" She pushed her forehead as close to the crack in the door as she could, but the angle was wrong and she still couldn't see the front door.

Mom and Dad do have lots of friends. At least they're not like the mean kids who throw rocks at the windows, or shouted bad things from between the willows.

From her dark hiding place she peered through the three inch opening for the first to enter the foyer. Her wait was short, for in stepped a pretty blond lady almost the same age as her mother. She slowly looked about the place and then promptly closed the closet door.

"Very good job, Birmingham," she said. "You and Mrs. Emily have certainly made this an easier day for us all."

"Yes, ma'am." Birmingham smiled, looking back at Ralph.

"You gonna stand there all day?" Ralph stared back at the handy man with raised eyebrows.

"Ohhh." Birmingham quickly picked up his two boxes and eased into the foyer.

"Birmingham?" spoke the blond lady from the living room.

"Yes, Mrs. Heather."

"Take the china right into the kitchen. I'll deal with that first."

Susan eased the door open again. There was yet another person there right behind the one Birmingham called Mrs. Heather.

"Mrs. Crutcher," grumbled Susan under her breath. "What is the Wicked Witch of the West doing here now? Every time she comes, she brings strangers and they stay much longer than they should." She watched Birmingham and the one called Ralph go back through the foyer toward the big yellow truck.

Susan peeped around the door, through the screen door, and out into the yard, knowing full well something else was afoot. Someone was shouting near the road, one whose voice sounded to her like fingernails scratching a blackboard.

Those awful kids from across the road. Molly Hatcher has brought her little gang of criminals with her and they're already taunting the newcomers from the willows.

"The Ghost of Weeping Willows," they sang, "won't visit you tonight, but she'll come and stand at the foot of your bed at first morning's light."

Susan could feel her face flush. Her anger built as they continued to sing and laugh.

"What are they singing?" Anna turned toward the willows from the open front doors.

"Something about a ghost," replied Hunter. "What is Weeping Willows?" He looked back at Mrs. Crutcher.

"Uhhh . . . It's just 'The Willows' dear. That's what the Christophers called this place. Mr. Clarence built it some time ago and then gave it to his son when his first child was born." Glancing at the kids between the willows, she grumbled, "There's no 'Weeping' to it." She walked briskly past Anna and stopped at the steps, eyeing the kids. "Get out of here, you little cretins!" she shouted. Waving her hands about, she scattered them away from the lower grounds. Looking back through the doorway, she added, "I'm sorry, Mrs. Elmore. You do have good neighbors, but kids will be kids. When you get all settled in and they get to know you, all that will stop I'm sure."

"What of the ghost?" Hunter stood smiling at Mrs. Crutcher.

"Bosh and bunk," she snapped. "There's no such a thing." She looked to Heather again and the scowl quickly vanished. "My glazier has been kept quite busy replacing the windows these little misfits have broken. I'm quite sure now that they know someone lives here we'll not have another visit from him."

Heather smiled. "I'm sure Brice will be intrigued. He has a thing for ghosts."

The smile on Hunter's face quickly garnered a cold stare from Mrs. Crutcher.

"You're lucky to have such a good husband," replied Mrs.

Crutcher as she pulled her gaze away from Hunter's smiling face. "I think you all will be very pleased with The Willows. It's really quite a find. Not many agencies like ours would let such a house go so easily with forty acres of prime farm land." She walked over to the grandfather's clock by the fireplace, stopped, and then turned to face them. "This old Hamilton, the furniture, and everything else comes with it you know. This old clock behind me has been in the family almost as long as the house has been standing."

"But . . ." Hailey stepped close to her mother and looked at Mrs. Crutcher, "why would they just let all of this go? Don't they have any family?"

"Ohhh I'm certain they know of it, but they are quite well off. I guess, for one reason or another, they didn't want a thing." She turned to Heather. "I'll be telling my employer that you're getting settled in and are very satisfied with The Willows." Looking at the old grandfather clock, she added, "It's got an eight day movement and chimes quite loud, but I'm sure you'll enjoy it. It keeps perfect time."

"Who kept this place up?" Anna ran her hand over the fireplace mantle. "Birmingham said that it hardly needed dusting and the old clock was wound, oiled, and working."

"Ohhh . . . yes," stuttered Mrs. Crutcher. "My employer has a maid who visits here every two weeks or so. She must wind the clock too. It runs a long time you know."

"I see." Anna noticed the brass plate mounted below the face of the clock. *Eight Day Movement.*

Heather smiled. "I'm sure we'll like it, Mrs. Crutcher. Can't wait to start on the gardens." She turned to Hailey. "Please check on Hunter. I don't think he's in his room and I don't see him anywhere. I don't want him poking around in that old barn until Birmingham checks it out."

Looking very pleased, Mrs. Crutcher added, "This has worked out very well, Mrs. Elmore. The Willows was just waiting for the right family. I'm very happy you are pleased with it." She glanced out of the open front doors. "I see the van backing closer. I'll just get out of the way and let you and your family set up the house."

"I'll see you outside." Heather closed the closet door again. "Brice has stored some of our furniture. For the love of me, I don't know what we're going to do with what he's got on that moving van.

Right family? Susan eased the door open once

more and peeped out through the crack. *My father will fix this just as soon as he gets home.*

As she listened to the 'Wicked Witch' leave in her Volkswagen, she began to hear something else—something that made her eyes squint, something that brought fingernails and blackboard back to mind.

Molly Hatcher. Easing the door open a little wider, she quickly looked from the foyer to the living room.

Nobody here now.

Susan spun around and looked through the screen doors and on past the porch. Everybody was milling around the little silver pickup and the big yellow van. But what was more disturbing, was the sight of the same little group of kids. They were now clustering up just across the road from her iron gates.

"They're not coming here," she grumbled at a whisper.

Little delinquents.

She balled here fists up and shut her eyes tight.

♎ ♎ ♎

In a flash she was among the flowing branches of the willows. She could instantly feel the breeze move their tentacle-like limbs against her hair, face, and shoulders.

"Come, you scaredy cats." She could also hear Molly dare them on.

Susan slowly opened her eyes, and peered through the limbs. She was in the willow on the west side and looking toward the other willow and the iron gates. She could, once again, feel the heat building in her face as she pushed through the limbs, across the open area, and on to the far willow.

She's starting something again and pulling that Sanders boy right into the middle of it. I thought I was rid of 'Our Gang'.

Molly pointed out the big, brass lock dangling

from the hasp. "They left the gate wide open." Looking back at the other five kids, she asked, "Who's coming with me to The Willows? We might just meet the next, brave souls who try to live there."

A brown-haired boy of ten or so stepped forward with a half-smile, his freckled face marred by a frown. "You're fixin' ta mock that ghost again, Molly Hatcher." His voice stern. "Hasn't last Halloween taught you anything at all?"

"Of course not, Jimmy Sanders," she snapped. "That paint can was an accident, pure and simple. The wind just blew it from one of the shelves."

"Yep." He giggled, causing muffled laughter from the others. "I guess it was the wind that opened it on the way to your head wasn't it?"

The other kids giggled loudly, drawing a frown from Molly.

"Well, Jimmy," grumbled Molly, "you can stay here with the other 'kids' if you want. I'm sure they are just as scared as you are."

The grins held on the faces of the others, but not one stepped forward. Molly shook her head in disgust, letting her gaze drift back to Jimmy.

"I'll go. I'll go," he managed reluctantly. "But I'm not goin' much past that first willow."

"Good." Molly turned to one of the youngsters. "Vicky Passeur . . ."

The buzz-cut, tow-headed ten-year-old cringed. His eyes grew big.

"You stay right here and watch for that Mrs. Crutcher's VW. I don't want her running us off in front of the new-comers."

Vicky let out a soft sigh of relief as he nodded. He knew full well that he was out of the picture.

"That Molly Hatcher . . ." Susan's knuckles turned white as she watched her and Jimmy walk across the gravel road and toward the gate.

Susan pushed her way through the thick limbs until she was at the far edge of the willow. About ten paces from the iron gates, she glanced back toward the house. Everyone was busy with boxes, pictures, and other things they were taking from the van.

"Just to the edge of the first willow," whispered Molly.

Susan turned to see her coaxing Jimmy through the gates, and then on to the edge of the first willow where he promptly stopped.

"I'm not going any farther," complained Jimmy. The frown was back.

Molly glanced back at him, smiled, and then recited a little poem.

"Come, brave souls of Willow road
and stand 'neath the willow trees.
Wait for the ghost of Weeping Willows.
She'll visit there indeed."

She smiled at him again.

Jimmy squinted. "You're doing it again," he whispered. "If you recite one more of those stupid poems, you'll be standin' here by yourself."

But Jimmy's eyes weren't the only pair squinting.

Susan eased forward. "I'll give you a poem you won't soon forget." She pushed through to the edge of the dangling limbs to about an arm's reach from Jimmy.

"Hear that?" Jimmy's eyes grew big. Looking to his left, he tried to see through the gently moving limbs of the old willow.

"Hear what?" Molly looked back at him, and then to the willow.

"Someone said somethin' and it wasn't me." He shivered.

Rubbing his arms, he watched his breath swirl

into the air. "See that? See that smoke?" He slowly backed from her. "For cryin' out loud, Molly Hatcher, it shouldn't be cold here."

"No-you-don't!" Molly grabbed the front of his shirt. "It's still spring for Pete's sake. You just hear the leaves of the willow rustling in the breeze."

No sooner had she said that, than Jimmy's eyes grew big and his chin dropped to his chest.

"What's got your goat now!" she snapped.

"Shhh," he hissed. "Just listen."

The voice spoke soft and quiet, but now seemed to come from between them. It was a poem Molly was not familiar with.

"Come, Ghost of Weeping Willows.
Come and stand by me.
I'm not afraid of your cold, dread breath,
and I'm not afraid of thee."

"Ohhh crimmany," groaned Molly, closing her eyes tightly.

Feeling Jimmy's shirt jerk from her grip, she opened them quickly. He had left in such a hurry, she only glimpsed the back of his shirt as he ran through the iron gate.

Perhaps it was the peculiarly, cold breeze that finally moved Molly, or maybe it was the shouted words, "Don't come back!" that did the trick. At any rate, the words she screamed as she followed Jimmy's path, garnered the attention of those now working at the van. They stopped to watch her as she ran past Jimmy, down the road, and away from the house.

Susan stomped her foot. "Good riddance," she grumbled. She then closed her eyes tightly and thought of her own bedroom. At that very instant, she was swept from the willows, and toward that very place.

♎   ♎   ♎

Opening them again, she was pleased at the sight of her own bed. Instantly plopping down upon it, she buried herself in the midst of her pillows. No sooner had she done that, than she heard another troubling sound—someone was on the front porch.

Again?

She sprang up, ran to the head of the stairs, and then crept down them one step at a time. Eyeing the big brass door knob, she could see it being twisted back and forth. Then, as a blurry figure presented itself on the far side of the frosted glass doorway, she got a distorted view of the interloper.

The colored man again?

Her eyes grew big as the door knob clicked. With little time to think, she flew down the stairway, passed the front door, and then straight to the coat closed on the far side. She was so quick, she hardly had time to open the door. Now in the dark, she turned the door knob and eased it open ever so slowly just as the front door opened.

You're back again? Is everything in that big truck going in here?

She watched the one called Birmingham pause barely inside the room, holding two more, large boxes. Although there was another, older white man behind him, also with boxes, the colored fellow refused to move any farther. He looked right at the closet, back at the white man, and then all about the large entranceway.

"For Pete's sake, Birmingham, you're doing it again. These boxes are heavy," grumbled the white man. "Go on! Those boxes go into the dining room. Mrs. Elmore is coming up the steps right behind me."

"Yes sir, Mr. Ralph." He through an uneasy glance back at the tall, trim, slightly gray-haired fellow. "I saw somethin', Mr. Ralph. I know I did. It zipped right passed those frosted windows as I started to open the door." He squinted at the coat closet but said not a word.

Birmingham eased inside, constantly eyeing the stairway and the closet, but stopped again just inside the doorway.

"What's got into you?" complained Ralph. He pushed passed the handy man, walked through the foyer, and then on into the living room. Once there, he sat his boxes down and looked back at Birmingham. "Are your feet glued to the floor? We've got a van to unload. Mr. Elmore's off to buy something for supper, he'll be back any minute. I'd like us to have a sizable dent in our load when he gets here."

"Right." Birmingham eyed the partially open coat closet door, pushed it closed with his foot, and then eased on into the living room.

"It just will not stay shut," explained Heather Elmore as she walked into the foyer with a load of boxes also. "I noticed it when I first looked at this place. I'll have you take a look at it a little later after we get settled in."

"Uh huh," agreed Birmingham, eyeing the door becoming ajar once more. He giggled. "I know I shut it. I heard the lock click, but there it goes again."

Heather shook her head and continued with her boxes.

"Ohhh, come on, Birmingham." Anna passed him with a big box and paused to look back. "Paisley carpets, heavy-looking curtains, antiques everywhere, and a fireplace you could stand in. Don't make this old place any more spookier than it already is. You'll have Hailey sleeping on the front porch. Besides, I kind of like the change." She promptly sat her boxes on the couch to the left of the front door and trotted on passed it to the first bedroom.

"Awwwwwww." Susan rushed from the closet, dashed across the foyer, and then raced up the stairway.

The crashing of china at Birmingham's feet sent rigors up Ralph's back. He quickly looked up from his boxes, spun around, and then glared at Birmingham. The handyman's two boxes now lay on the floor. The closest one to the floor looked seriously damaged.

"Greek Gods, Birmingham!" snapped Ralph. "What in the devil is wrong with you now?" He glared at the ruptured corners of the bottom box. "I don't even want to think of what's in that box."

"I'm most sorry, boss." Birmingham looked from the stairway and back to Ralph. "Somethin' ran right behind me. I heard it groan. I know I did. Then, when I dropped my boxes, I saw it go right up those stairs." He nodded toward the stairway. "It was movin' so fast, all I could see was a blur."

"Have you been . . ." Ralph walked over to him, leaned close, and then sniffed.

"I have not. No, I haven't. I swear I haven't," exclaimed the handyman. "My wife left me with two dollars for today and I'm not much on cheap Ripple wine. It's sicknin' sweet and tastes like cough syrup."

Heather knelt by the box. "Just don't touch anything else marked fragile. I'll take care of them and these two also. Go back to the van and get the boxes marked bedroom number three. That's up the stairs to the left. Anna and Hailey will be in that one."

"Upstairs?" Birmingham swallowed hard, glancing at Ralph. "It would be." He grumbled on the way back to the van.

♎   ♎   ♎

Meanwhile, Susan lay upon the bed closest to the window with her face buried in her pillows. "It can't be, Igon," she sobbed, clutching a little, brown Teddy bear. "It just can't be. They're doing it again and Mom and Dad are not back yet."

A long time gift from her grandfather, the Teddy was old, faded, and had one, left, eye button missing. It had always been there for her—a comforter or confidant whenever she felt sorrowful or undone. But just as the face of her grandfather formed in her mind, something bumped the bottom of the bedroom door. She quickly rolled to her back. Clutching Igon, she lay as still as she could, watching the door slowly open.

"Don't tell me I didn't feel anything," grumbled Birmingham as he backed through the door, grappling with two, huge boxes. "Don't tell me I didn't feel anything, either," he added as he lay the boxes in the middle of the room. He paused, looking at the beds. "Uh Oh." His voice weak. "All the other bedroom doors were open—beds straight and neat and rooms nice and fresh. Now, just look at this— bed covers wrinkled, place smells like honeysuckle, blond hair in the hair brush, and finger prints on the makeup mirror." He looked back to the far bed. "And what's with that old Teddy bear?" He gradually backed toward the doorway, eyeing the bear. "That's OK," he added, forcing a grin. "I know you here. Jus' remember, the Elmore's live here now and Miss Anna and Miss Hailey don't need anything else sharin' this room with them."

He stopped just outside the door, still eyeing the bear. Just as soon as he did, the door slammed itself shut.

"Uh huh." He turned and briskly walked toward the stairway. Once he got there, he continued down the stairs.

"Birmingham?" came the page from the living room.

"Yes Ma'am, Mrs. Elmore, I'm comin'. I'm really comin'."

Heather turned and walked to the front porch with the handyman right behind her. "You were raised in the country, right?" She stared back at him.

"Yes, Ma'am. One of eight more."

"Will you do me a very big favor and find Hunter for me.

I've lost him again and I just know he's in that big old barn. Tell him if he doesn't get back here and unpack his things he can sleep on the floor with the mice."

"Mice?"

Birmingham stared at the barn. The two-story building looked sound enough. Its one-by-ten boards were still in place as were the four-by-ten sheets of galvanized tin on the roof. But Father Time had all but erased the color of the cypress. It now had a grayish-green hue and the windows offered a distorted, wavy view of everything on the far side.

"Just find him for me," continued Heather. "Mrs. Emily is putting your stuff in the servant's quarters right now.

You'll have three rooms, and a nice kitchen and bath."

"Yes, Ma'am." He hesitated, thinking of the old barn, waist-high weeds in the front pasture, and what was in them. "So much for this city boy," he mumbled as he stepped from the porch.

"Hurry now," prompted Heather, now standing at the van.

"It's already noon and I'd like to get this thing unloaded before one."

"Right away, Ma'am."

Birmingham hastened his steps across the freshly

mowed front yard, but quickly faltered when he got to the cattle gap.

"Just thirty yards more," he said, eyeing the tall Johnson grass, hog weed, and goldenrods. Sidestepping through the 'V' shaped gap, he looked toward the barn again. "That boy gonna be the death o' me yet—grass tall enough to hide most anything, barn a hundred years old, and one o' the big, front doors wide open. Yep, he's in there all right and catchin' God only knows what." Looking closely at the weeds, he noticed a fresh path and it went straight toward the open door. "Uh huh," he added weakly. Easing forward, he pushed each and every tall weed away from him as he passed. "Chiggers, grandma." He jumped, thinking of the little, red, and itchy spiders. "Hunter!" he called as he approached the barn. "Is you in there? Mrs. Heather is havin' a conniption. If you don't come out o' there with your hands empty, you won't be able to sit down for supper."

No reply came from the barn.

"Uh huh." Birmingham hesitated just steps from the doorway. "Who told me that life would be less eventful in the country?" He eased up to the partially open door and peeped into the darkness inside. *Got to be at least a dozen events hidin' in there and watchin' me right now.* "Hunter!"

"Up here, Mr. B."

The reply came not from a ladder on the left of the barn's open space, but from above it in the darkness.

Hay loft. Birmingham eased forward, past the tack room, and on to the wooden ladder made into the wall.

He watched uneasily as the dust filtered down from the cracks in the loft flooring. First on the left side, and then across to the right side it went.

Backing away from the dust, he looked up again.

"Hunter! What is you doin' up there?"

"Stay there, Mr. B."

Hunter's reply came almost as a warning, stopping the handyman in his tracks.

"Don't move, Mr. B. If he knows you're down there, it'll be harder to get him out of the loft."

"Him?" Birmingham moved close to the ladder and stared up toward the tin-covered roof. "Hunter! What is you chasin' now?"

"Gopher snake, chicken snake, or a reticulated rat snake I think."

"Ritka, Ritiku—a what?"

"I just need a closer look. He's a really good one—about ten feet long."

"Ten feet!" Birmingham wiped the sweat from his brow with his right sleeve and gazed back into the darkness of the loft. "I jus' heard your father drive up. They'll be puttin' lunch on the table any minute."

"There! I got em' by the tail!" exclaimed Hunter. "Just have to work him out from between these bales."

The old handyman beat violently on the ladder. "You turn that critter loose right now, Hunter! If you take that thing to the house, Mrs. Heather gonna faint dead away and I'll be already dead right here. Now get down here right now!"

"But—"

"Right now!" Birmingham pounded the ladder again, punctuating his words. "My pants done got bag-a-lice all over em' and cockle burrs wound all up in my new sox. Good Lord only knows what's in my britches. Now come down here this very minute!"

"But he's tame." The sound of something being drug across the loft floor toward the top of the stairs quickly moved the handyman away from the ladder.

"Nothin' that big is tame, Hunter Elmore," answered Birmingham, still backing toward the front doors. "He's just savin' his energy to bite the pee-waddled-in-squat out o' you. Now, turn that serpent loose and come down here right now or I'm goin' after Mr. Brice. You got fifteen seconds to get down here with them hands empty."

Waiting patiently, Birmingham heard something hit the hay and perhaps a bare part of the wooden loft floor.

"That sounded awfully big, Hunter. Let me see your face at this ladder right now, this very minute."

Hunter leaned over, grabbed the ladder, and then looked down at the handyman.

"Your fifteen seconds are up, little man. You get down here right now," demanded Birmingham.

"Awww, Mr. B," complained Hunter as he gingerly stepped down the ladder. "What's the good in living in the woods if you can't catch stuff?"

Birmingham slowly shook his head. "Young fella, you had best grow some brains. You keep this up and before long, somethin's gonna catch you. What's your mother gonna do when she finds you in the front yard, half-swallowed by some big, boa-python thing?"

Hunter laughed loudly as his feet hit the barn floor. "That's two kinds o' snakes, Mr. B. And they both live in Africa or somewhere way off." He turned from the ladder, smiling at the old handyman. "You're scared of this place aren't you?"

"Not exactly. Jus' ain't learned to love it yet." He pointed toward the open front doors. "The house is that way. You got work to do on your room. Do you want to sleep on the floor with the mice and spiders?"

Hunter reluctantly walked past him and on toward the doors. "Awww, Mr. B, that room already has a bed and even a cabinet for my clothes."

"That's a shift-a-robe, and you still got to unpack 'em, so get to steppin'."

Part 2
Can You See Me?

Susan lay quietly in the bed nearest the window and listened to the sounds coming from downstairs. Doors opening and closing, muffled voices, and things being shuffled about worried her. But the constant bumping of those now unloading the big van outside, proved to be an almost intolerable distraction. Each time someone came close to the bottom of the stairway, she sat up and look toward her closet. That was the only place that made since right now. It was her refuge, her safe-house, her hiding place, and she knew it all too well. Then, as the little, porcelain clock on her nightstand showed 4:00pm, she heard voices of people coming up the stairs and they weren't the least bit familiar.

Ohhh nuts!

She sprang from the bed and shot into the closet, leaving the door slightly ajar. Hearing the door knob snap, and the bedroom door opening, she barely had enough time to spin around and peep through the tiny opening at the intruders.

Sisters?

Two, young girls walked inside—one, pretty blond about seventeen or so, and one of auburn hair, quite cute, and about thirteen. Then, she repositioned herself to see the third. She was a much older colored lady.

She must be Mrs. Emily, a maid perhaps.

About five feet and six inches tall, the colored lady's hair was pulled back in a very tight, four inch bun. Hitting heavily upon her heels, she walked straight to the bed closest to the window and jerked the covers from it. Igon the Teddy bear went flying across the room to the far, left corner.

"Ohhh!" flinched Susan.

The blond stopped immediately, looking at the younger sister. "What?"

With raised eyebrows, the auburn-haired girl looked up but offered not a word. They both then turned toward the colored lady. She was standing at the bed, arms full of linens, and staring at the closet.

Nuts again. Susan eased away from the door to the far right corner and her waiting safety blanket she had kept since a baby.

Seeing the door slowly open, she held her breath and closed her eyes tightly.

"I don't see a thing," said the blond, glancing back at the other two still quite near the second bed. "There's boxes of stuff in here, a few clothes, a box of Christmas ribbons and stuff, and someone's pink and blue blanket on the floor." Looking back to the clothes hanging to her left, she surmised, "This was a little girl's room. It's a shame she wasn't a boy. She seems to have been about the same size as Hunter."

It's still my room! Susan leaned forward for a closer look at the blond.

Although Susan's eyes were now open, and her anger justly kindled, she still remained reluctant to be heard.

"Just forget it, Anna," spoke the maid as she gathered the sheets and spread from the remaining bed. "If I get these on the line quick enough, you can use 'em tonight." They're really in good shape."

"Thanks, Mrs. Emily." The auburn-haired lass pushed at the mattress close to the window. "I like this one, Anna. It seems good enough."

"Fine, Hailey." Anna turned from the closet and looked to Mrs. Emily. "We'll take care of this room right now. Where is Hershey?"

"Who knows where that chocolate Lab is right now. I 'spect he's with Hunter, chasin' rabbits or somethin'. He'll be here, sniffin' 'round shortly, I suppose."

"Anna. . ." Hailey squinted at the make-up mirror, desk, and chair. "You can clean that thing up. You're the only one who'll use it. There's smudges on the glass and hair still in the brush."

Anna paused at the mirror and picked up the brush. "Did you use this thing?"

"Nope." Hailey smiled. "We just came in. Remember?

"There's hair in it."

"Just throw it away." Hailey barely afforded it a glance.

"Auugh!" complained Susan from the closet.

"I don't think so," decided Anna. This looks to be silver with an ivory handle. You can't find this kind at the five and dime." She looked up at the mirror. "There's fingerprints all over the glass too."

Susan wiped her wet cheeks as she backed away from the door. Closing her eyes, she thought of the old barn.

♎ ♎ ♎

The scent of hay immediately greeted Susan as well as the hard top of the old feed box she was now sitting on. She eased her hand to the wood, feeling its roughness.

Smiling, she slowly opened her eyes. "I wish Mom and Dad were back now."

A cold rigor traveled up her spine to the very top of her head. She was not alone. Something very big and brown was sitting directly in front of her and only feet from the box she was on.

"Ohhh wow." Her voice soft. "Are you a Shepherd? Maybe you're a wolf. But I've never heard of a brown wolf before.

You certainly are a big fellow, aren't you?"

Hershey cocked his head, but still held his eyes on her.

Susan eased down from the box, watching his big, brown eyes follow her.

"Can you see me?"

Hershey blinked once and jumped to his feet. The soft woof made her smile and certainly answered the question.

"You can, can't you?" She took a step toward the Lab, stopping when he raised his ears. Susan looked through the partially open doors and toward the house. "Did you come with the little family who say they're moving in?"

The chocolate Labrador eased closer to sit down only a short step away. A single tear tracked its way down her left cheek and dangled from her chin.

"If that's so, then. . ." She paused, looking into Hershey's eyes. "I truly now think that my Mom and Dad don't live here anymore. Does that mean something happened to them? Does that mean something happened to me?"

Hershey immediately got up, stepped forward, and then liked her face, removing the tears completely.

"Wow." Susan gently pushed the big Lab back. "Aren't you the friendly one. You like to run?"

Susan eased to the doorway with Hershey right behind her. The smile upon her face widened—even more wide than it had been in a great while.

"I must warn you right now. I can run really, really fast."

Hershey woofed one, sharp time and then jumped back as if daring her.

"Very well then, my pretty friend, let's see if you can keep up."

Sprinting from the open doors, Susan flew through the hogweed and Johnson grass so fast the four-foot weeds hardly moved. But the big Lab was right behind her, barking and jumping gleefully.

"That's it, boy! You're really fast yourself!"

♎ ♎ ♎

At that same time, near the chicken coop in the lower end of the back yard, Birmingham eyed a huge Rhode Island Red rooster. It had taken up its post in the doorway and was now eyeing him suspiciously.

"Go on now!" Birmingham waved his hands at the big rooster. "No one has to get hurt here."

Clucking and strutting nervously, the rooster held his ground, eyeing the handyman.

"You are still too close to the door. Go and chase a grasshopper or somethin'," he added, stomping his feet. "Miss Heather wants eggs for potato salad. I jus' need 'bout six. Now, go on and leave me have 'em."

But just as Birmingham took a step toward the doorway, he noticed something leaping and jumping through the weeds toward the cattle gap.

"Hershey?"

He watched as the brown Lab stopped abruptly, seemingly looking up at something in the V-shaped gate.

Slowly turning, he watched the dog intently. "You been chewin' on wild-wood weed or somethin'? What you lookin' at?"

Hershey zig-zagged though the gate and headed into the back yard. With eyes widened and feet glued to the ground, Birmingham watched the big Lab jump and run here and there until he disappeared around the west side of the house.

"Can't be . . . No-it-ain't." He slowly turned, facing the darkness of the coop. "No Saturday should start like this."

"Birmingham!" Heather stood looking out through the screen of the kitchen window.

"I got 'em. I got 'em," he replied.

Checking the west side of the house once more, he peered back inside the coop, checking for the rooster.

♎ ♎ ♎

Feeling strangely diminished somehow, Susan stopped in the front yard and looked toward her window just above the porch roof. Smiling at Hershey, she shut her eyes tightly and thought of her 'safe spot'.

♎ ♎ ♎

The slight smell of mothballs and the scent of cotton brought a quick smile as Susan opened her eyes. The comfort of darkness always pleased her and was seldom duplicated by much of anything else lately. Rubbing her blanket as if stroking something alive, she turned and eased to the closet door. Kneeling upon her right knee, she gradually twisted the big, crystal knob, pushing the door slightly ajar.

They're still here, Igon," she whispered, glancing back at the old Teddy Bear sitting upon her blanket, tightly tucked into the corner. *They're putting stuff in boxes. . . . My clothes?*

Anna picked up three or four dresses, folded them, and then gently placed them into one of the boxes. "There's probably a lot of stuff here the orphanage would like to have. I heard Dad say the family let just about everything go with the house."

Susan immediately looked over her right shoulder. Both closet rods were bare—not a hanger on them. *"How can this happen? Where is my father? I know my mother wouldn't ever leave me."*

Then, as tears began tracking their way down her cheeks once more, a familiar shade of brown flashed by the crack in the door.

"Hershey!" spoke someone from the bedroom.

That was Hailey's voice. Susan moved slightly so as to see the younger sister. Smiling, she watched her ruffle the Lab's ears, kissing him atop his head. Susan's smile widened. But the big Labrador was not distracted by his little master at all. He was staring right at the crack in the closet door.

Susan's smile widened, whispering, "So you belong to the girls. I've made a good friend of you, perhaps it wouldn't be too hard to do the same of your masters."

"Ohhh no you don't." quipped Anna as she pushed the closet door closed. "You're not sniffing around in there. You'll run out something that'll make us all leave." Squinting her eyes, she fanned the air slightly. "What's that smell?"

"Honeysuckle." Hailey nodded toward the dresser. "There's a bottle of it on the makeup dresser.

Susan slowly twisted the nob, pushing the door ajar once more. The Lab's ears perked up. "Hershey?" she whispered. "So that's your name."

The Lab barked loudly. Quickly standing, he pointed the closet like a Spaniel.

"What's your problem, boy?" Anna looked toward the door. "It's open again, isn't it?"

"Ohhh . . ." Susan scooted back to her blanket just as Anna opened the door wide and peeked inside.

Hershey squeezed between Anna and the door, stepped inside, and then sat down, staring right at the blanket.

"You can see me, can't you?" whispered Susan.

The Lab's ears quickly fell and then shot right back up as if awaiting something else from the cute, little stranger.

"Lands-o-mercy." Mrs. Emily came in the room clutching another set of linens.

As Anna backed up, Susan could see the colored maid as she started making up the first bed with Hailey's help. "Get that hound out o' there. He's after a mouse or somethin' worse. This place got Birmingham so nervous he won't come in here, hardly go near the front door, and now there's somethin' in the back yard."

Anna eased up by the Lab, scratching his head. "That honeysuckle scent is in here also." She reached down, took hold of the corner of the blanket, and then jerked it from the floor.

"I'll take that." Mrs. Emily grabbed the blanket, folded it, and then placed it with the dresses in the box. "Father Jones will be pleased a peas when Mr. B takes those boxes to St. Christopher's tomorrow."

"Ohhh. . ." Susan froze, looking at what Hershey was now hanging on to. Igon was hanging by a paw from the corner of his mouth.

"Hershey!" she whispered, as quiet as her excitement would allow.

But the Lab was now following the maid toward the bedroom doorway.

Pausing at the doorway, Mrs. Emily looked back. "Mr. B said there was somethin' a bit unusual 'bout this room, but he didn't mention the closet. I think that Mrs. Crutcher's been lettin' this place out to somebody on the sly."

She turned and headed toward the stairway with Hershey right behind her.

Hailey looked to her big sister. "What do you think of the closet?"

"Oooo. . ." Anna wiggled her fingers out in front of her. "There's no such a thing as ghosts." Nodding toward the makeup mirror, she added, "There was a child here though. Look at those handprints." Anna stepped close to the mirror. "About six or seven I'd say. Mrs. Emily was probably right. Mrs. Crutcher was probably renting this place out by the day." She vigorously wiped the glass. "It's almost 8:00 PM. Let's get our clothes on the racks. You take the left and I'll put mine on the right. This is our place now and it's up to us to make good with it." She looked back to Hailey. "No more ghost stories."

Back in the corner of the closet, Susan watched the first handful of dresses come in. Wiping the tears from her face, she closed her eyes once more and thought of the big, white oak in the front yard near the porch.

♎   ♎   ♎

The cool breeze and rustling of oak leaves told her she had got her wish.

"Ohhh providence," she said, looking down at Hershey.

He was lying upon the front porch next to Birmingham, sitting in his old rocking chair. Igon lay between the paws of the big Lab.

"Hershey?" Birmingham paused, looking at the family pet. "Wish you could talk. I'd sure like to know what you were dancin' about the back yard with. Maybe then, I'd be more at peace with this place."

Susan eased out on a big limb, closer to the two just below her. She eyed the little, brown bear intently. Hearing the rustling of leaves, she looked down at a little chipmunk near the trunk of the tree. He had also garnered the Lab's full attention.

Don't look up. Don't look up. Susan eased all the way out to the last leaf.

Then, with all the silence of a falling feather, she drifted down toward the little bear. Quickly grabbing it, she kicked off the edge of the porch and shot toward the roof. With one, quick bark, Hershey leaped toward the bear. But his snap fell short and the bear disappeared above the roof.

The smile now pinned upon Birmingham's face looked absolutely out of place. He was completely frozen, gazing up toward the roof.

Easing from his chair, he glanced at Hershey and then looked back toward the roof. "Dog . . . I know you can't talk. But, just for me, please tell me you threw that thing up there." He slowly turned, stepped to the edge of the porch, and then looked up again. "Ain't commin' down is it?" he managed. "Fine," he whispered, walking toward the front door. "If my bed ain't ready, I'll jus' wrap myself in a blanket and lay down on the floor."

♎   ♎   ♎

Susan closed the crack in her closet door and eased back onto her blanket. Placing Igon back in his corner, she looked at the faint light coming from under the door. There were people still in her room and also someone walking from the stairs toward it.

"Mrs. Emily, we have just about finished in here," spoke a familiar voice from the bedroom.

That's Anna's voice. I know it. Susan sat up.

But as she eased toward the door, she could hear another, strange sound. Something was sniffing, very near the floor, and just outside the door. Resisting the urge to turn the knob, she eased closer to the door and listened.

"What's got your attention now, Hershey?"

That's Hailey. A faint smile visited Susan's face. *If her hair was a little lighter, we'd look like sisters.*

Outside the closet, Mrs. Emily put her hands upon her hips, staring at the girls. "I don't think I'll guess what you two are up to. I have cold cuts, fresh tomatoes, sliced cheese, and fresh bread on the table right now. You two need to eat a little somethin' before you turn in. Don't, and you'll have nightmares for sure. Goin' to bed on an empty stomach jus' ain't healthy."

Back in the closet, Susan peeped through the keyhole. "Mrs. Emily," she whispered and then jumped as Hershey scratched at the bottom of the door.

Easing back to the keyhole, she tried to get a look at the sisters again, but the persistence of the Lab proved most distractive. "They do seem awfully friendly," she whispered as she pressed her cheek against the floor for a better look at the family pet. "Shhh, Hershey!" she whispered.

But that only excited the big Lab. He jumped back, lowered his head to his paws, and awaited his new, friend to jump out at any moment.

But Hailey's patience was up with the Lab. "Mrs. Emily!" Hailey's tone seemed awfully angry as she squinted her eyes at Hershey. "Please take Hershey downstairs. I don't want him scratching up the door. We'll be down right away."

"Yes, Miss Hailey."

♎ ♎ ♎

Later that evening, Anna and Hailey sat upon their beds, listening to their radio. The stress of the day had put them low in their pillows, almost to the point of dozing for Anna. The house was mostly quiet with the exception of Hunter's room. The tinkling of metal could be heard now and then, heralding the collapse of yet another of his Erector Set inventions. Anna, in the bed closest to the door, yawned heavily, marked her place in her book, and then laid it upon the nightstand between the beds.

Hailey propped herself upon her right elbow, looking at her sister. "May I read some in your book?"

"It's 'Southern Haunts' and a little scary." Anna forced a little smile.

"I've been warned," quipped Hailey. She grabbed the book, fluffed up her pillows, and then settled in on the beginning of the anthology. "More interesting than scary, I think, but I'll leave the lamp on."

"Have it your way," came the sleepy warning as Anna rolled toward the door.

Not to be distracted, Hailey turned off the radio and turned to the first short story, 'Hell's Gates'.

Back in the dark of the closet, Susan heard the radio go off. But there was still a dim light coming in from the bottom of her door. Creeping up to the door knob, she gingerly twisted it and eased the door open a bit. The top hinge squeaked eerily causing her to stop immediately.

Hailey lowered the book. Smiling, she replied, "Let's not forget to tell Mr. B to fix the closet door and oil its hinges."

A weak "Whatever" was all Anna managed.

Seeing no sign of brown fur, Susan opened it a bit further, but there was no squeak.

Good. One asleep and one reading. And . . . I think the right one. She looks friendly enough—much better than the handyman. He won't stand still long enough.

She tiptoed to the foot of the bed and reached for the headboard. But her little hand slipped through the wood and she felt not a thing. Tiptoeing, she could see a tuft of brown hair slightly above the book. Seeing she had not yet disturbed her hopeful friend, she floated from the floor, drifted over the footboard, and then paused just behind the book.

Now or never.

Holding her right, index finger as stiff as she could, she poked at the book.

Nothing. Her finger slipped right through the hard cover.

Suddenly, Susan froze as the book came down to show Hailey rubbing her nose. But she just cast a suspicious eye at the bottle of honeysuckle perfume, slowly shook her head, and then raised the book again.

Whew! Susan took a deep breath, stiffened her finger again, and then tried the book. Nothing. Again she tried, and then again. Finally, upon the fifth attempt, the book moved, gravity immediately recognized mass, and Susan plopped upon the bed, sitting upon Hailey's legs."

"Wha . . ." Hailey's face, wide brown eyes, raised eyebrows and all finally came into sight.

Susan quickly put on her best smile. "Can you see me?"

"Yeeooow!" Hailey flung the book at the strange, blond girl, jumped from the bed, collided with Anna trying to get up herself, and then fell to the floor with her sister.

"What is it?" shouted Anna as she watched her sister spring to her feet, and run from the bedroom.

Anna looked back at the open closet door and then to the book in the floor at the foot of the bed. "Hailey! What in the world is wrong with—"

"Guess I scared her, huh?" spoke someone from Hailey's bed.

Anna slowly looked from the book to the one now standing upon the covers of Hailey's bed.

"Ohhh," replied Anna as the room faded to black.

♎   ♎   ♎

"Miss Anna! Miss Anna!"

Anna gradually opened her eyes to see her sister peeping over Birmingham's right shoulder.

"Take this and wipe her face." Heather handed the handyman a wet face towel.

The cool towel felt good and comforting somehow, leaving Anna staring at her sister. "Did you see her?" Anna squinted.

Hailey, not saying a word, only glanced at her mother.

"My, my," replied Birmingham. "Let's not go into that kind of thing right now. How do you feel, Miss Anna?"

"Fine." Anna stood and sat upon the edge of her bed. "Just overextended myself I think. I'll be all right with a little rest."

"Good." Mrs. Emily sat a glass and water pitcher upon the night stand. "If you feel weak again, I've got some Castoria in the medicine cabinet. A little cod liver oil will do you good now and then."

"She'll be fine. I'll watch her." Hailey stepped around Birmingham and sat upon her bed also.

"Good," replied Birmingham. "We'll leave well enough alone and go back to bed too."

Watching the last one leave the room, Hailey glanced toward the closet and then whispered, "Please, tell me you saw her."

Anna nodded slightly. "Six years old, blue eyes, and blond hair just like what we found in the brush."

Hailey's eyes grew big. "I heard her. She asked me if I could see her."

Anna stood, looking at the closet door, now closed. "Just before I passed out, I heard that door close."

Hailey eased her feet to the cold, maple wood floor, turned, and then tiptoed toward the closet.

"What are you doing?" Even through the excitement, Anna could hardly hold her voice down as she followed her sister.

"Are you kidding?" Hailey's eyes fixed upon the door. "This is the best mystery ever. It's more exciting than the snake that got into our last home, and it stayed hidden for a week."

Hailey twisted the knob and carefully opened the door.

"I don't see a thing," whispered Anna. "But . . ."

The seventeen-year-old's voice trailed off leaving her staring at something in the darkness.

"But what?" Hailey nudged her younger sister.

"There, in the far, right corner." Anna pointed out the blanket and bear. "I didn't put that there. Did you?"

"No. The last time I saw the bear, Hershey took it from the room. The blanket is supposed to be in the box with the clothes and stuff."

Easing the door closed, Hailey turned to her sister. "Who do you think knows the most about ghosts and such in our family?"

"Birmingham, of course. He's the only one of us who ever talks about them."

Hailey glanced at the clock on the nightstand. "Nine fifteen. Do you think they're still up?"

"Sure." Anna grabbed her housecoat. "They both watch the news and weather. That's not over until after ten something."

"Good." Hailey grabbed her housecoat and looked to Anna for the first move.

Smiling, Anna led her sister from the room, down the stairs, and then on toward the back door. The short distance across the back porch left them at the back door of the servant's quarters.

Anna peeped through the window. "The light's on in the kitchen. They're still up like I thought."

Knocking loudly, they both waited for a sound from someone inside.

"I'm comin'. I'm comin'. Jus' a minute please."

"That's Birmingham." Anna stepped back from the door.

Finally opening, the handyman looked down at the two on the other side of the screen door. The fuzzy collar on his purple house coat perfectly accented his red house shoes.

"Very chic," quipped Anna, obviously amused.

Birmingham shrugged. "Can't find mine yet." Opening the screen door, he added, "Guess they're still packed away somewhere. What can I do for you two this time o' night?"

"We have a question." Anna glanced back at Hailey. "We have a kind of mystery and we'd like you to help us with it."

"Spooky mystery," added Hailey, grinning.

"Uh huh." Birmingham stared at the two as if over imaginary glasses. "Why am I not surprised?" he added weakly.

"Shouldn't be," started Anna. "We know as well as you that something weird has been going on ever since you first set foot in this house."

Birmingham grew strangely silent, but the stare was still there.

Hailey eased to her sister's side. "I believe we saw what, or who, you said Hershey was playing with in the back yard today. We think she's the same one who made you drop the china."

"Ohhh boy." The old handyman rolled his eyes. "Not real sure I wanna know."

"Ohhh come on, Mr. B," complained Anna. "This is more fun than any old TV show. With a little time in the library records department, I'll bet we could find out who were the first owners of this house."

"Stop—just stop." He briskly rubbed his face with both hands. "One thing at a time. First, and I can't believe I'm askin' this, what was it that dog was chasin' earlier today?"

Anna's smile widened. "She's a little girl—blond, blue-eyed, and about six years old."

"You've lived her longer than we have," added Hailey. "Do you remember who lived here back then?"

Birmingham scratched his head, looking up toward the ceiling as if for help. "Mrs. Mary and Mr. Lionel Christopher, I think. He owned a little grocery and a bakery right next to it. It sat on the north side of Main Street almost to the east end." He looked to Anna. "I know they had a child, but not much else."

"She died." Mrs. Emily walked into the kitchen, pausing at the stove. "Some say she died right here in The Willows. That's why they call this place Weeping Willows. Seems she had a bad fever and it got the best of her late one Saturday afternoon. The Mr. and Mrs. gathered her up, ran to their automobile, and then raced toward old Dock Hall's home. The paper said they blew a tire, lost control of the car, and then went over the bridge at Non Conna Creek. The vehicle turned upside down in about four feet of water. Not a soul survived. They found them the next morning."

"My oh my." Anna's gaze lowered to the floor. "Would you know the little girl's name?"

"Not sure. Only saw her once. About five or six maybe. Pretty little cotton top though."

"Blonde?" Hailey glanced at her sister.

"Yep." She gestured toward the back door of the main house. "Go up them stairs. When you get to the top, instead of turnin' left to your bedroom, turn right. You'll see another bedroom, but we turned it into a storage room. When Mr. B and I first cleaned it up, we found a ton of books, picture albums, and framed pictures. We knew they would probably mean little to your parents, but we jus' couldn't throw 'em away. Didn't seem right somehow. Mrs. Heather finally dusted them off and stacked them on a table in the far corner. Some of the bigger pictures are leaning against the wall nearby the door."

Both the girls, looked at each other, spun around, and then headed toward the back door.

"Wait a minute." Birmingham put a hand upon Heather's right shoulder, turning her around. "You two saw somethin', didn't you?"

Hailey looked to her sister and then back to the handyman.

The nod from Birmingham was almost nonexistent, but there nonetheless. "You did. You did see somethin'. You're not makin' this up." He turned and walked toward the living room. "My, my. I think I hear Detroit callin' my name."

Mrs. Emily stepped close to the girls. "No foolishness now. Tell me the truth. I heard your mother say that Birmingham saw somethin' when he carried the first of the boxes into the house. Whatever it was made him drop the dishes."

"We think he did," replied Anna, "and we're going to prove it."

The two sisters ran from the servant's quarters, into the main house, and then headed toward the stairway.

"Shhh!" hissed Hailey. "Mom and Dad are probably in their bedroom. They might not like us snooping around those things up there."

"Right," agreed Anna, already halfway up the stairs.

In just seconds, the two were at the storage room door, staring at the lock.

"The key's in it," Hailey glanced at her sister.

"I'm not so sure this is right." Anna's voice weak. "What if the little girl doesn't want us poking around in her things?"

"Don't be silly." Hailey grabbed the key, turned it, and then eased the door open. "We've already boxed up all of her clothes and stuff. How personal is that?" She opened the door a little wider and peeped inside. "This was a playroom, not a bedroom." She flipped on the light switch and then nodded toward something painted on the floor directly in front of them. "That's a hop-scotch game. It goes all the way across the middle of the room. Look at the end of it."

An old, painted rocking horse stood at the end of the game, right in front of the room's only window.

Anna stepped around her sister and slowly walked to the center of the room. "Mrs. Emily and Mr. B really did a nice job cleaning this place up." She gestured to the left wall. "I'll bet the little girl's picture is in one of those old frames, or somewhere on that table in the left corner. I'll bet—"

"No need," interrupted Hailey as she stepped up beside her sister.

Hailey's gaze was locked on a little, triangular table in the far, right corner. Upon it sat one, eight by ten, gold framed picture.

"It's her!" Anna ran straight to the table, stooped down, and then looked almost afraid to touch it. "Blond hair, blue eyes, and about four years old in this picture." Carefully picking it up, she held it up to the weak bulb dangling from the center of the ceiling. "Something is engraved upon the bottom of the metal frame. "Susan A. Christopher and Igon."

"Ohhh wow." Hailey eased up beside her sister. "So that's Susan."

"Yep. And that faded, little, brown Teddy bear in the closet is her Igon." She looked at her sister with a smile. "She doesn't seem so spooky now, does she?"

A reserved "No." was all she could get from Hailey.

"We need to put this on our night stand."

Hailey squinted. "Are you kidding? Mr. B's been talking about Detroit all day. If he sees that picture, he'll be packing his bags for sure."

"Don't worry about that." Anna carefully wiped the glass with her right hand. "I don't think Mrs. Emily will let him do that. Besides, when Susan sees this, she'll know that we like her. I think she needs help getting to where she needs to be. She's kind of stuck here somehow and can't do that by herself." Looking at Hailey, she added, "What do you think?"

"I guess so, but how do you go about helping a ghost?"

"Haven't figured that part out yet, but I'm sure it'll come to us."

Ω   Ω   Ω

The next morning, Hunter awoke listening to the

strangest sound he had ever heard. To him, it was like the 'Call of the Wild' novel all over again.

Rooster!

He kicked the covers off, swung his feet to the side of the bed, and then quickly sat up.

"Awww nuts. It's Sunday."

Running on the balls of his feet to the door, he slowly eased it open. There was nobody in the living room and he didn't hear anyone in the kitchen.

We don't have a church here? Maybe there is no church way out here anyways.

Then, almost as predictable as Christmas, a mental picture of the old barn presented itself. Spinning around, he ran to the bed, picked up his grass-stained blue jeans from beside his shoes, and then hurriedly jerked them on. Socks, shoes, and a T shirt found their way to their appropriate places on the way to the back door. The only thing that would distract him now was the aroma of Mrs. Emily's blueberry muffins, but there was no one in the kitchen to formulate that barrier. He stared at the stove, but it was as cold as yesterday's biscuits setting atop it. Hearing his mother and father moving about upstairs, he quickly pulled his mind away from the blueberry muffins.

"Hershey!" he called, trying not to be too loud.

Not getting a response, he gingerly opened the door, stepped out onto the porch, and then eased it back shut again. But just as he turned toward the barn, he noticed someone open one of its two, big doors and step inside.

"Who-is-that?" He paused, but the little, blond-haired girl didn't step back outside.

In but seconds, the youngest of the Elmore clan was stepping through the V-shaped, cattle gate and trotting through the tall weeds toward the partially open doors of the old barn. Pausing in the early-morning shade of the old wild pecans, he peered inside the dimly lit barn.

"Hello," he said loudly as he stepped toward the doors.

Susan, glancing down at the lad from the barn's hayloft, kept pushing her finger at one of the posts supporting the tin-covered roof. She could almost feel it—just enough to make a slight sound.

"Please-please-please," she whispered, noting that the feeling of the old post was becoming stronger and stronger.

Back down on the hay-covered floor of the barn's open space, Hunter turned one way and then the other, but he couldn't locate the direction of the weak thumping sound he was now hearing. As the sound became louder and louder, he looked up toward the hayloft opening.

"Hello?" He squinted into the darkness.

"Can you see me?" spoke a soft, girlish voice.

"Sure." Hunter squinted at the darkened silhouette standing in the loft opening. "I saw you from the house just a minute ago. I'm Hunter Christopher. We just moved in. Are you one of our neighbors?"

"Uhhh, yes. I guess you could say that."

"Come down." Hunter gestured toward the ladder to his left. "It's nailed to the wall, close to the tack room. My name is Hunter Christopher. What's yours?"

"Uhhh, Alice." Tapping the post again, she walked around the opening, pausing at the ladder. "Move back. I've got a dress on."

Grinning, Hunter slowly backed toward the still open double doors.

Resisting the urge to close her eyes, she gripped the ladder with both hands and then eased down its wooden runs step by step, watching the strange, little boy closely. "Your friend is still up here you know."

"Friend?" Hunter squinted.

"I saw you . . . I know you like animals."

"Ohhh." Hunter smiled. "You mean the big rat snake. I did catch him, you know, but our handyman made me turn him loose."

Susan paused at the bottom of the ladder. "How do you like my dress?" She spread out its pleats.

"I like yellow, and buttercups too. It looks great. I think my sisters would like it also. Have you lived here long?"

Susan smiled, staring at the open doorway. Hershey was sitting there, looking at her intently. "I was born here, actually."

She leaned toward Hershey, softly patting her hands together. The big Lab immediately trotted up to her, closed his eyes, and then buried his face in the front of the dress.

Susan knelt and hugged him. "He feels so . . . warm and soft and healthy and alive."

"He eats from the table you know. Sometimes, Mom gives him Gravy Train. Looks like you're dressed for church. Guess we'll find one once we get settled in."

Susan matched his smile. "Thanks. When my Father and Mother get back, I want to be ready to go." Stepping a little closer, she added, "I really like your family. The last two families that visited here didn't stay long. Some of them were rude and drank too much. When they started seeing things, they left. Besides, they didn't have girls or pets like Hershey."

"Seeing things? What things?"

"Here, Hershey," called someone from somewhere near the house.

The Lab quickly looked toward the open doors.

"That's my sister, Anna," explained Hunter. "Guess it's Gravy Train time. Nobody's cooked breakfast yet."

"Go, boy." The little blonde girl gestured toward the door.

Without the least hesitation, Hershey bounded from the barn and out the doorway.

"Come." Hunter reached for her hand. "I'll introduce you to her."

"Uhhh." Susan backed up. "I really have to go now. I've been here far too long I fear."

"Very well. Just wait right here. I'll be right back."

Hunter spun around and ran toward the door. Quickly pausing at its opening, he looked back, but the strange little girl was nowhere to be seen.

"Alice!" He looked to the ladder and then toward the loft opening. Turning toward the back doors, he noticed they were still bolted. "Alice?"

♎ ♎ ♎

Meanwhile, after feeding Hershey, Anna joined Hailey on the front porch. Each had a pan and there was a bushel bag full of dried corn between them, still on the cob. . . .

"I didn't know chickens could be so much trouble," grumbled Hailey, pulling at the dry husks of her first ear.

"Just husk it and I'll shuck it," offered Anna. "My grip is a little better than yours. We'll get Hunter to feed them. He's not getting out of this 'chore' thing."

"Get me to do what?" Hunter walked around the edge of the house, eyeing them suspiciously.

"Work. You big gold brick," grumbled Anna. "You're helping us with this chicken thing."

Hunter slowed to a stop at the steps, looking at his two sisters. Anna's comment was more of a demand that an answer to his poorly timed question.

Hailey glanced up from her pan. "Everybody has chores, Hunter. Now, we have more of a farm than just a home. We make the chicken feed, you feed the chickens, and Birmingham collects the eggs. Got it?"

"Sure . . . I guess." Sitting down on the top step, he added, "I just met one of our new neighbors. Her name is Alice. She was in the barn."

Anna squinted. "Barn? It's not even 9:00 a.m. yet. What's someone doing snooping around in our barn this time of the morning?"

Hailey froze with both hands still gripping a corn cob. "What did she look like?"

"Ohhh, my age I suppose—yellow hair, and blue eyes. She was dressed for church in a pretty, yellow dress with—"

"Buttercups all over it?" Hailey dropped the partially shucked cob in her pan.

"How did you know?" It was Hunter's turn to squint. "You've already met—"

"That was the last dress I put in the box!" Hailey all but dropped her pan to the porch floor.

"I know. I saw it." Anna quickly stood, staring at her brother. "Did it have an embroidered white collar and cuffs to match?"

"Well, the collar was white all right, but—"

Hailey slid her pan toward the steps. "Feed the chickens. We've got to check on something."

Hunter picked up the pan. "What's all the fuss? There's hardly any feed here."

"Just something we've got to check on," answered Anna as she followed her sister back into the house.

Almost running up the stairs, the two sisters dashed into their room only to stop at the big box in the corner to their left.

Hailey approached it as if something was about to jump out at her. Slowly opening the box, she froze. "It's gone. The yellow pleated print is gone."

Anna quickly turned, walked briskly to their closet, and then slowly opened the door. "Ohhh

Hailey." Her voice weak.

Hailey eased up beside her sister. "Your dresses are on the left and mine are still on the right. So, what's the pro . . ."

Hailey's voice trailed off as she noticed four other dresses. They were hung in the very back of hers and just above the little, pink blanket in the corner.

"I see them, Anna." Hailey's voice weak also. "There's a little, blue dress, a pink one, and a brown one." She turned to her sister. "Hunter saw the yellow one, didn't he?"

"Yep," whispered Anna. "She has it on. Hunter has not only seen her, he has also talked to her."

The two backed away from the closet, closed the door, and then sat down upon their beds eyeing one another. At that very moment, Hershey came trotting into the room, visited them both, and then sat down directly in front of the closet.

"She's here," whispered Anna. "What are we going to do?"

"Help her of course. But how?"

Part 3
All Alone

Later that afternoon, Anna and Hailey sat in one of the swings on the front porch staring at the framed picture of Susan they had found upstairs. Birmingham was finishing up an additional swing to the left of the front door. Done, he sat down in it and eyed the two.

"My, my," he complained, forcing a slight smile. "I can hear them wheels turnin' from here. What are you two conjurin' up now?"

"We need your help, Mr. B," replied Anna.

"Well, here I sit. There's my tool box. What can I fix for you today?"

"It's not really for us." Hailey held up the picture in her lap. "She's here, Mr. B. You know about ghosts and spirits and things like that. How can we help her?"

Birmingham's jaw dropped and his eyes grew big. "My, my. I had to ask." He shut his eyes, briskly rubbing his face.

"You know about her, don't you?" Anna touched the gold frame. "Did she really die here?"

"My, my." Birmingham closed his eyes again and eased his head to the back of the swing. "Most say she did. Right up there in what is now your bedroom."

"We've seen her." Hailey sat up. "Hunter saw her this morning. I believe he even talked to her."

Birmingham briskly rubbed his mostly bald head. "That Mrs. Crutcher knew this place was haunted. The only thing she said 'bout the others is that they tried to stay here but they weren't comfortable with the place."

"What are we going to do to help her?" asked Hailey.

"We!" Birmingham jumped to his feet. "There is no 'WE'."

He rubbed his face and head again. "When I was a kid, even younger than you two, my Aunt Lucy died. She left us the house and we moved into it that very week. There was eleven of us in that big, five bedroom home. You do the math." Taking a half-step toward them, he looked down at the picture. "I still have dreams of somebody, who ain't got no body, sittin' down on the side of my bed and leavin' me with nothin' to see." He looked up to Anna. "I suggest it's time to get your father involved it this little mystery of yours before it gets bigger than all of us." Walking to the screen door, he paused, holding the handle. Finally looking back at the girls he added, "Your mom is takin' you three to register at the schoolhouse tomorrow. Better get some rest. From then on, you'll be takin' the school bus, I think."

"Uhhh." Hailey flopped back down in the swing.

♎   ♎   ♎

The next afternoon, after the rigors of registration, Anna, Hailey, and Hunter sat in one seat of the bus eyeing all of the strange faces. With few names to go with them, they sat there still and quiet, pondering their fate. It was hot and dusty on the gravel road, but with every window on the bus open, at least there was a good breeze. Anna sat staring at the back of Molly Hatcher's head. Through Molly's eyes, she now had a much different view of the lovely, old home they had just moved into.

"What are we going to do?" whispered Hunter.

"We will not be intimidated or scared off." Anna glanced at her siblings. "The Willows is still a very beautiful place. It just has a resident who needs our help."

Molly glanced back at them. Her smile angered Anna almost to the point of words. But before she could reply, the bus slowed to a stop.

"Willow View Avenue," announced the driver.

Molly stood, glancing back at the three Elmore kids.

"She won't turn down our street?" asked Hailey.

"No, silly." Molly smiled at the others. "It's just a hundred yards or so. There are few houses past us and none with kids. A little walk won't kill you."

Anna, Hailey, and Hunter joined the other four as they walked down the aisle toward the door. Anna slowed, but said not a word. The other two knew she was dodging Molly, but that didn't work for long. When the red-headed know-it-all stepped off the bus, she turned with her arms crossed and waited for them with her partner in crime, Jimmy Sanders.

"Bye Mrs. Narbie," said Molly melodically as the Elmores stepped from the bus.

The driver waved politely, promptly closed the doors, and then rolled off in a puff of blue smoke and dust.

Jimmy stared at Anna with one of those 'I know something you don't' smiles. "What bedroom do you sleep in?" finally came the question.

"The big one upstairs," replied Hailey, noting that her sister was reluctant to answer.

"Sleep well last night?" Molly now had conjured up the same smile.

"Never better," replied Anna with no hesitation at all.

Walking up the road behind Molly and Jimmy, Hunter nodded toward several other kids waiting under the old Sycamore in front of Molly's house. The iron gates of the Willows were still another thirty yards past it on the right.

"She's still there, you know," poked Molly without turning around.

That brought a soft chuckle from Jimmy. "Tell

'em," he prompted.

Molly's smile widened. "She walks through the halls at night, waiting for her father to return. She's stuck there, Anna. She'll always be there waiting and waiting and waiting . . . with you all."

"Don't listen to her," grumbled Hailey.

"Look." Anna pointed toward the Willows drive in the distance. "There's Father's truck. He's already home."

Running around Molly and Jimmy, the three Elmores left their troubles standing in the gravel road in front of Molly's house and ran toward the black, iron gates of the Willow's lower grounds. Just as they entered the house, Anna spotted her father and mother sitting on the couch, listening to the radio. Anna wheeled from the door, dropped her books on the long table directly behind their couch, and then stood there waiting for one of them to turn around.

"Uh oh," Heather sat up, curled her long, blond hair over her right ear, and then smiled at Brice. "First day at school and Anna's hardly smiling."

Brice, with his eyes closed and head resting upon the back of the couch, refused to be torn from the newscast on the radio.

"Did everything go well for all of you?" asked Heather.

Anna stepped slightly forward. "Did you know that Mrs. Crutcher knew this place was haunted?" Anna's tone, although soft, was nonetheless demanding of an answer. "She had to. Every kid in the school knows about it—every kid but us."

Hunter slowly nodded.

"Ohhh, good grief." Brice sat up, looking back at Anna. "Why would you believe something like that?"

Heather moved to the edge of the couch. "You can learn a lot from what kids say. Most of them just repeat what they hear from their parents." She looked back to Anna. "What did you find out?"

"We have a little friend and she still lives upstairs, with us."

"Kind of 'lives'," added Hailey.

"Ohhh . . ." grumbled Brice.

"Birmingham has seen her," snapped Anna. She leaned slightly across the table. "He spotted her through the front door window the first time he put the key in the lock. Hunter has seen and even talked to her. She's the little Christopher girl, Susan. Mrs. Emily told us that she came down with a terrible fever one night. Her parents tried everything to break it but they failed. When they couldn't revive her, they panicked and tried to take her to the doctor. They both died when they lost control of their car and plunged into a creek not far from here. I think Susan actually died right up there in our bedroom that very day."

"She's still here, Father," added Hailey excitedly. "I don't think she knows her parents have died. She's been waiting, every day, for fifteen years for them to come back."

"Time continuum." Brice looked silently at Heather. "Actually, this does interest me," he finally said. He looked back to Anna. "You say that Hunter saw her?"

"We saw her also. She was just as real looking as you are right now."

"I see. . ." Brice's gaze drifted toward the open, front door. "I am very angry at Mrs. Crutcher. She knows that our company investigates things like this and relocates families who have this problem and yet she laid it all right here in our laps." Brice stood and walked to the front door. "I can't imagine someone who would maliciously set up family to endure such a thing. I'm going to have a word with her right now."

"Ohhh, Brice." Heather quickly stood. "We all

love this, old place." She glanced at the kids. They were nodding their approval. "I don't want to—"

"Move?" Brice smiled. "I don't really want to, either. I was thinking that Mrs. Crutcher might know the whereabouts of some of Susan's relatives. With a little luck, some might still live close enough to visit. If she thinks I'm about to lay this place right back into her lap, she might be a bit more helpful I'll bet."

"That's good." Birmingham opened the screen door, looking at Brice. "I didn't get a good look at her when we were moving in, but I did hear her." He nodded at the stairway. "She all but flew up them stairs when I did, and she sounded 'bout as sad as a body could get. That is, even if she had one. Actually, she was just a gray puff o' smoke when—"

"I see," interrupted Brice. Rubbing his chin, his gaze finally made its way to Heather. "I'll try her on the phone. If I'm not satisfied with that, I'll go to her house. She'll think the sale is in jeopardy and will try anything to help us."

"Is it, I mean. . ." Heather glanced at her daughters. "Is our home in jeopardy?" Heather's voice low.

"Not a chance," smiled Brice. "This is our home now. But we must try to help Susan right now if we can."

♎ ♎ ♎

Later that evening, and with her father's success in finding where Susan's grandparents lived, Hailey reclined upon her bed. Opening Anna's book once more, she felt completely at ease with her father taking such control of the situation. The little clock upon the nightstand between their beds read 9:20 pm. The radio had already put her sister to sleep again and the music now playing was a bit too country to listen to. Hailey rolled over and checked on Hershey. He was lying between the beds, sound asleep also. So far, he had not even glanced at the closet.

A little noise is better than none. She turned the radio down a little and returned to Anna's book.

Time passed, and now the little clock read 10:15 pm.

"Girls, you've got school tomorrow," came her mother's lights out warning from the base of the stairs.

"Yes, ma'am." Hailey plopped the book back upon the nightstand and promptly turned off the lamp.

Ten minutes later, Hailey had found her comfortable spot. She was just about to drift off to that second star on the right when a soft woof caught her attention, completely chasing drowsiness from the picture. Slowly rolling to her right, she peeked down between the beds at the Lab. His head was upon his left paw, eyes open, and staring right at the closet. Thoughts of sleep flew from her as quick as a fly from the swatter. Hershey gradually moved his head. He looked to be following something from the closet to the far side of Hailey's bed—something that no human could readily see.

"What the . . ." Hailey froze, noting the sudden tightness in her bottom sheet along with a slight movement in her covers to her left.

Looking toward her sister, she could only see a little puff of blond hair sticking out of the quilts. Hailey's gaze gradually made its way down to the family pet. Hershey's head was up and looking right at her, but she knew that it wasn't herself he had in mind. Hailey eased back to her pillows, staring at the ceiling. The room was almost without light, save for what the moon could give through the partially open drapes.

She's friendly. She's friendly. Perhaps just one more look.

Ever so slowly, she rolled her head to the left. She could now plainly make out the little, elongated lump in the covers at the far edge of the bed.

"Ohhh nuts." Her voice weak.

Gathering up what little nerve she could muster, Hailey eased her left hand under the covers and on toward the lump. Inch by inch it slid between the cool sheets, clinging to the last bit of courage she could dredge up. Then, just when it was about half way, a little hand slid into hers. It was icy cold, but very soft nonetheless.

"Susan?" Hailey managed at a whisper.

Maybe it was Hailey's fright, finally edging to terror that defeated her nerve, or perhaps it was the little giggle from the lump that did the trick. At any rate, it sent Hailey screaming and kicking from the covers, stumbling over Hershey, and finally launching herself toward Anna's bed.

"What-what-what?" Anna instantly awoke, pushing herself back upon her pillows and against the headboard.

"She's here! She's here!" screamed Hailey, bouncing upon the lower part of Anna's bed.

Amid the screaming and Hershey's loud barking, Anna tackled the nightstand, finally found the lamp's switch, and even managed to turn it on. Quickly wiping her eyes, she promptly retreated back to the headboard, looking all about the room.

"What in the world is going on with you now?" Anna stared at her sister, still standing upon the foot of the bed.

"There-there," managed Hailey, holding out a shaking finger toward her own bed.

Only then did Hailey realize that the 'lump' was gone.

"There's nothing there, Hailey, but. . ."

Anna's voice trailed off as they both looked toward

the Lab. He now looked as if he was the only one calm in the room. But, once again, he was staring straight at the closet.

"She's here," whispered Hailey, nodding toward the closet.

All of a sudden, the bedroom door burst open sending the sisters grabbing for each other.

"Are you two all right?" Brice stood just inside the doorway with Heather right behind him.

"We heard you all the way downstairs." added Heather, looking about the room also."

Brice pushed his brown hair back from his face and stared at Hailey. "What's going on now? You look like you've just seen a . . ." He raised his eyebrows. "Well, did you?"

Hailey studied her father's expression. "Would it please you if I said we did?"

A smile gradually curved its way around the right corner of his mouth. "I suppose, maybe."

"Well . . . I should really say it was more like I felt one this time." Stepping from Anna's bed, Hailey paused right in front of her father. "The first time I saw her, I was in my bed, reading a book. I felt her get in. I lowered the book and there she was—just as close as you are right now. Just a minute ago, I felt her get into my bed again. I felt her move the covers and saw the little lump she made in them." After glancing at her sister, she looked down at the floor. "Father, I'm afraid I messed up and completely wasted my chance. She put her hand in mine and I panicked. When I felt her cold hand, I could lay still no longer. All that screaming was mostly me. Susan and Anna may have added to the noise, but I couldn't tell right then."

Brice's eyebrows raised once more. "And she is our Susan Christopher as we suspected?"

Hailey nodded. "I'm sure of it."

Anna jumped from the bed and joined her sister. "Father, you've helped so many people." She quickly grabbed the picture from the nightstand and returned to her sister's side. "Can you not help us?"

Mr. Elmore stared intently at the face of the little blonde in the picture. "This is, perhaps, the first time I have ever been personally involved in a project." Looking up at his daughters, he added, "I'll do my best. But in the meantime, are you two all right?"

Hailey nodded reluctantly. "Anna's more comfortable with this than I am, but I believe we'll be fine."

"We'll just leave the light on," added Anna.

♎   ♎   ♎

The next day, a Tuesday afternoon, Anna sat on the couch in the living room, working on her homework. Finally, she closed her notebook and rested her head upon the back of the couch.

"I'm no good with math right now." She glanced at her mother. "I can't seem to concentrate. I can't get what is happening between our family and our little guest out of my head."

Heather smiled. "I wish I could help you, sweetie. This is your father's territory and I don't know a thing about it. But, on the other hand, you have got your father's attention. I don't think Susan is a threat to anyone in our family, but the thought of having a real ghost in our home simply gives me the willies."

As Heather was speaking, a knock sounded upon the door.

"I got it." Birmingham walked briskly from the dining room, straight to the door, and then opened it.

Anna listened, settling back upon the couch.

"May we see Anna please?" The voice wasn't entirely unfamiliar.

Molly Hatcher? Anna plopped her workbook down on the coffee table and looked back at Birmingham.

"A visitor for you, Miss Anna." Birmingham stepped to one side and motioned for the two to come in.

And Jimmy Sanders. Anna stood, speechless.

"Take them upstairs," suggested Heather. "Show them to the library and Birmingham will bring you and your guests some refreshments."

"Ohhh good." Molly looked toward the head of the stairs as Jimmy did an eye roll toward Anna.

"I don't remember a library in this, old house," added Molly.

"It was Susan's playroom." Anna led them toward the stairway. "Birmingham has been working on it for us. We had boxes of books with no places to put them. Birmingham made the shelves before we moved in and we've finally got most of them placed."

"Go on." Birmingham nudged Jimmy toward the stairway. "The place looks completely different."

"Right," grumbled Jimmy. Slowly trailing behind the girls, he looked back at Birmingham. "Don't you need some help or something?"

"Not at all."

With a gentle hand on the young man's back, Birmingham headed him on toward the girls. The young fellow shook his head as they neared the stairway.

Birmingham eased closer to Heather. "That's some o' Anna's troublemakers and window breakers."

But just before the little group got to the top of the stairway, Hershey trotted out of the girl's bedroom and stopped at the head of the stairs, eyeing the two visitors. His low growl instantly told Anna that he had already met her two guests.

Molly stopped abruptly. "So this is where you live?" She stared at the big Labrador. To Anna, she added, "I didn't know you had a coon dog."

Jimmy giggled.

"Hailey!" Anna called loudly.

Hailey stepped out of the playroom with a handful of books.

"Would you please take Hershey outside? I don't think he likes our guests."

"Wonder why?" Hailey sat her books down upon a small, hall table. Eyeing the two in disbelief, she took hold of the Lab's collar, and led him past the two.

Hershey constantly looked back at the Hatcher girl all the way to the bottom of the stairs.

Once at the bottom, Hailey looked back at Molly. "Are windows the only thing you throw rocks at?"

Molly ignored the comment. Jimmy never made eye contact. He kept looking toward the bedroom on the left at the end of the bannisters.

"Is that it?" he finally asked without looking away from the room.

"It what?" Anna stared at the two from the top of the stairway.

"Uhhh. . ."

"Susan Christopher's room of course, silly." Molly stepped up by Anna, still eyeing the partially open bedroom door. "There's a window in there that the ghost looks out of from time to time. She's been seen there more than a dozen times and not just by kids."

Anna frowned. "Watch your manners, Molly Hatcher," she snapped. "It seems to me that you and your little group knows very little about Susan Christopher. If you woke up tomorrow in a big, old, empty house and couldn't find your family, what would you do?"

"That would be scary," admitted Jimmy, earning a cold stare from Molly.

"That's not gonna happen," answered Molly smugly. "My family loves me."

Anna threw her a slight frown. "Come with me,

Molly." Anna led them to the play room/library, pausing at the open door. "Her family loved her also." She gestured inside the room as she entered.

"We heard of it." Molly's voice weak.

Seeing Molly and Jimmy were reluctant to enter, Anna paused just inside the doorway. "We're keeping some of the pictures. Most of them are of Susan. Birmingham has dubbed this place, 'Susan's Library'. Seems to fit, somehow." She nodded toward the far window and the brightly-colored rocking horse. "We're keeping that also. Susan evidently loved it very much. Birmingham pointed out the worn rockers and paint worn off of the hand grips on each side of the head. Her little knees also wore the finish thin on each side of the saddle."

"Why Anna," said Molly sarcastically, "One would think you've fallen love with someone who doesn't even exist."

Anna slowly turned back to see the slight smile on Molly's face.

Jimmy giggled silently, looking at Anna. "Ask her about the paint can last Halloween."

"Shut up, Jimmy Sanders," snapped Molly, punctuating the order with a sharp backhand to his midsection. "That was the wind, pure and simple."

"Right." Jimmy turned, muffling his giggles with his left hand.

"Be nice," reminded Anna. "There's no place for rudeness in this house." Anna stepped to the doorway to check the stairs. The handyman was nowhere in sight. Walking to the head of the stairway, she added, "You two can look around the library. Mr. B's got most of the shelves up. History and nonfiction is on the right. Fiction and adventure is on the left. Dad has a Science Fiction and Horror section, but it's still in the boxes close to the rocking horse. I'm going to help Mr. B. We'll be back in a minute or so with the refreshments." Pausing at the head of the stairs, she looked back at the two, still outside the library door. "Don't go snooping. Show some manners. This place is not a museum."

Molly watched Anna bounce down the stairway, turn, and then proceed on toward the kitchen. She stood silently, glancing at Jimmy with her hands behind her.

"I don't like that grin, Molly Hatchett," grumbled Jimmy. "What are you conjuring up now?"

Ω Ω Ω

Anna paused at the kitchen doorway, watching Birmingham gather what lemonade and cookies he could readily find.

"Hurry, Mr. B," she prompted, looking toward what she could see of the stairway. "Having those two in here is like shaking up a soda pop. Sooner or later, something's gonna happen."

"I got it. I got it." Birmingham quickly followed Anna toward the stairway with the refreshments. "Uh oh." He looked to the head of the stairs. "Where they at?"

"Susan's Library."

Anna, almost in a trot, hurried to the library door. Pausing at the entrance, she immediately noticed Jimmy sitting upon one of the couches in the middle of the room. The sheepish look upon his face, along with his unopened book, immediately screamed "Molly's into it again!"

"I knew I shouldn't of—"

"I told her to stay here!" blurted out Jimmy. "I really did. But she doesn't listen to anyone."

"My-my-my." Birmingham sat his tray of cookies and lemonade upon the coffee table between the two couches and looked up at Anna.

Even before Anna could say a word, she could hear Hershey outside on the porch. Barking and howling, he was clawing at the screen as if his life depended on it.

"This is NOT good," complained Anna.

She threw a quick glare at Jimmy and then trotted out of the library with Birmingham right behind her. Jimmy stopped at the head of the stairs, peering down toward the commotion Hershey was making. But as Anna and Birmingham continued toward her bedroom, a series of screams from the open doorway stopped them cold.

"Miss Anna! Miss Anna!" Birmingham took hold of Anna's right forearm. "You don't wanna go in there right now. Please. Miss Molly's done went into the closet. Let's just—"

But before Anna could make any kind of decision at all, the sound of ripping screens stopped the two barely a step from the bedroom doorway.

"I can't hold him!" shouted Hailey from downstairs. "Here he comes!"

Anna and Birmingham jumped to the bannisters and looked down on the stairway. The big brown Labrador was already halfway up the steps and disposing of the rest of them, three at a time.

"Stop him before he gets to us, Mr. B!" directed Anna.

"What!" Birmingham spun around, took three steps toward the head of the stairway, and then tackled the family pet.

Listening to scuffle behind her, Anna raced back and into the bedroom. Seeing the closet door was shut and Molly was still screaming inside, Anna grabbed the doorknob. But it was so cold that she could not hold onto it.

"Help, Mr. B!" Molly quickly pulled her right shirt sleeve down and tried the knob again. "It's frozen and I can't turn it!"

The rumble and screeching in the closet sounded

as if the two cats were fighting.

"Hold this animal!" shouted Birmingham.

Anna glanced toward the door to see the handyman running toward her. Hailey now had hold of Hershey, but it looked as if it was taking all she had to keep him from the bedroom.

"Move!" Birmingham brushed Anna aside and gripped the knob.

With the sound of cracking ice, the lock released the door, sending Birmingham falling backward into Anna, leaving both of them on the floor between the two beds.

The old handyman hardly had time to make it to his feet before Molly charged out of the closet.

"Look out!" screamed Birmingham, falling again back to the floor with Anna.

Hailey pulled Hershey away from the door as best she could and watched Molly run screaming from the bedroom and toward the head of the stairway. Her hair was in more tufts that one could readily count and it looked as if each one was tied with brightly colored Christmas ribbons that flowed six feet behind her. Hearing Jimmy scream as he hit what was left of the front screen door, Hailey finally let go of the family pet. He quickly scrambled after Molly, now at the bottom of the stairway.

"Why'd you do that?" asked Birmingham as he and Anna raced past her.

Hailey, sitting on the floor, rubbed her right hand where Hershey had twisted away from her. "Seemed like the right thing to do at the time," she grumbled. Struggling to her feet, she ran down the stairs, hoping to catch one more glimpse of the parade that just left their house. When she ran out onto the porch, her sister and Birmingham were standing near the steps, looking down the road toward town. Hershey had stopped at the front gate, but was still barking. Molly, on the other hand, had just about caught Jimmy and was showing no signs of slowing.

Heather stepped from the porch swing on the right, looking at Hailey. "What in the world is going on?"

"Just desserts," grumbled Hailey. "Anna," she added loudly, "let's check on the closet."

Seeing no response from her daughters as they ran back into the house, Heather turned to Birmingham. "What's got into those children and what in the world is in Molly Hatcher's hair."

"My, my," answered Birmingham weakly, still watching Molly run.

♎   ♎   ♎

Back upstairs, Anna followed Hailey into their bedroom, slowing abruptly as they entered.

"I got this." Hailey peered into the darkness of the open closet as she approached the doorway.

"I have nooobody," came a soft, voice from well inside the closet's darkness.

Hailey stopped, as did her sister. Neither said a word. The voice spoke again.

"I'm all alone and no one's coming for me. Strangers are now living and playing where I once did."

Hailey straightened up, leaning back against her sister. Every cell in her body was screaming "RUN!" but she didn't move an inch. Little by little, a shape began to appear in the far, right corner of the closet. Hailey began to make out the form of a small girl. She was sobbing softly with her forehead upon her folded arms, which were resting upon her knees.

"I see her," whispered Anna.

"Susan?" whispered Hailey.

It was not really a question, but a single word from a compassionate friend.

The little ghost slowly raised her head. Her

expression was one of sorrow, disbelief, and fear all rolled up into one little stare. Tears, streaming from her big, blue eyes, tracked their way down her cheeks, and then dripped from the bottom of her chin.

"You . . . You know me? You can see me?" Susan's voice quivered in the whisper.

Hailey's fear disappeared like steam from a kettle. She put on her best smile and nodded. "All in this house know of you, Susan Alice Christopher. Your picture is upon our bedroom night stand right behind me. We also feel your sorrow."

Gradually standing, a forced smile began to appear upon Susan's little, round face as she looked at Heather and Anna. But the sound of several people running up the stairway caused her to inch her way back into the shadows.

"Please don't go," whispered Hailey. "We're all friends here."

Anna turned to see her parents walk up beside Birmingham.

"I wouldn't," whispered the handyman. "There's somethin' in there that defies description."

Miss Emma eased up behind Birmingham and placed a hand upon his left shoulder.

"Shhh," hissed Anna. Looking at them all, she slowly shook her head as she mouthed "Susan is here."

"Told ya," whispered Birmingham.

"Wait, wait," begged Hailey, quickly placing both hands over her mouth. With tears welling up in her eyes, she turned to the group now very close to the closet door. "We were too many, or too loud, or . . ." She ran to her father, grabbing him. "I wanted you to see her, Father," she sobbed. "She's like a frightened little bunny and I don't blame her a bit! Can we not help her?"

Heather gently put her hand upon Brice's shoulder. "It's only seven. We still have a good part of the evening before us. I'll bet those at Rolling Hills are up also. Don't you think it's time to let them know what's been happening around here? After all, this concerns them as well."

"You've found her family?" asked Anna, wiping her eyes also.

Hailey quickly looked up into her father's face. "Ohhh father." Her tears began to flow again. "You've done this for others, why can you not help her right now?"

"I can," he replied softly as he rubbed the tears from her wet cheeks. "I think it is time to solve this little riddle. I would think at least one of her grandparents would come and see for themselves."

"Ohhh Father call them now," pleaded Hailey. "Please call them right now."

"I got 'em! I got 'em!" said Birmingham loudly.

Everyone turned to see the handyman hanging on to the big Lab's collar. It wasn't hard to figure out what he was looking at. The open closet was only a half-second from him.

"I forgot 'bout that front door screen," explained Birmingham. "He just came right in. I'll fix it right away."

Anna eased the closet door closed. "Let him go, Mr. B."

"Yes, ma'am."

Immediately, Hershey nosed by those at the door, trotted briskly to the closet, sniffed beneath the door, and then sat down, staring at the knob.

"She's still in there," whispered Anna.

"My, my," whispered Birmingham.

"That does it, Brice." Heather tugged at his arm. "Nobody sleeps tonight unless at least one of those Christopher's comes over her."

"My, my," complained Birmingham again. "I may never sleep again."

Part 4
Grandfather's Clock

Later that evening, Anna and Hailey lay in their room, listening to the radio. They could hear the old grandfather's clock in the living room strike eight times. Hershey rose to his feet, trotted from between the beds, and then paused at the foot of Anna's, looking toward the top of the stairway.

Anna sat up, looking at him. "I wish I could sense things like he can. He's not looking at the closet door anymore."

"Father said one of Susan's grandparents would be right along," added Hailey. "It's been an hour since and no one yet. Do you think they're—"

Before Hailey could finish her sentence, the heavy brass knocker sounded upon the front door. Scrambling as quickly as possible, the two girls grabbed their house coats and ran from the bedroom. Stopping abruptly at the top of the stairs, they peered down and into what they could see of the living room.

Birmingham had just shut the front door and was now looking at someone across the room. "Been right there ever since we moved in," he said to the person.

"He's looking at the clock," whispered Anna. "That's got to be Susan's grandfather."

"Come on, Miss Anna, Miss Hailey." Birmingham motioned for them. "Miss Emma's got a little somethin' for us on the table and we got a guest for dinner. Things been so hectic 'round here it's a wide-eyed wonder that she's had time to do anything." He met the girls at the bottom of the stairs. "Mr. Christopher is here. Came up in an old, red, fish tail Cadillac. Looks almost brand new."

"Thanks, Mr. B." Anna and Hailey walked toward the living room entrance way. "Hello," Anna said softly, noting the old gentleman was rubbing the face of the clock with his handkerchief.

Well into his seventies, and dressed in beige trousers, white shirt, and an English hound's tooth sport coat, he looked very dignified. He adjusted his round, wire-rimmed glasses, staring at the old Hamilton. Then, brushing his thin, corn silk colored hair back, he looked around at the three, still standing at the entranceway. Hershey had just eased up between the two girls. He watched the old fellow intently, but remained strangely silent.

Pulling his pipe from his vest, Mr. Christopher pointed the stem of the burgundy briarwood toward the clock. "Made her all by myself," he bragged, glancing back at the clock. Jackie wanted a fancy rosewood something-or-other, but I talked her out of it. Cost me a pair of French chairs to get her to let me make it. When we moved out, it seemed fitting to leave her here with my son and his family." Adjusting his glasses again, he smiled at the girls.

"We didn't hear you come in," said Anna.

"It's no wonder." He stepped to the fireplace and tapped the bowl of the pipe upon the hearth. "New shoes with gum soles," he added, pointing the stem of his pipe to the doe-colored, suede's amber soles. "What will they think of next?" He smiled, staring at his empty pipe. "Don't mean to barge in like this. Your Mr. Birmingham said I was expected."

"You are most expected," agreed Anna, as Hershey's tail began to wag with excitement.

"You came in from Rolling Hills, didn't you?" asked Hailey.

"Actually," his grin widened, "I came from here. Got this place some forty years ago."

Birmingham walked into the living room with a serving tray full of cold cuts, fresh bread, and cupcakes. "Hope somebody's hungry. I'll jus' sat this on the coffee table."

"May I sit?" Clarence looked at the handyman.

"And smoke also I suppose. Mr. and Mrs. Elmore will be down shortly." He placed an ashtray on the table next to the couch where Clarence had just sit down. Birmingham motioned toward the girls. "These lovely, young ladies are Miss Anna and Miss Hailey Elmore." Gesturing to the Lab, he added, "That fuzzy creature is Hershey."

"You all living here can call me Clarence." He looked down at Hershey. "Bet you've seen her, haven't you."

The Lab could hardly contain himself. But strangely enough, he made not the first move to approach the old gentleman.

Clarence stood and gently shook hands with the girls.

"I see you've made it." Brice walked from the dining area with Heather and offered the old gentleman his hand also. "Mr. Christopher, I presume."

"Mr. Brice and Mrs. Heather," prompted Birmingham.

The old fellow nodded, shook their hands, and then started stoking his pipe.

"Didn't expect to see you," added Heather. "I was under the impression that Mrs. Christopher was coming."

"Ohhh well." He smiled again. "The old hen always likes to run things. She seldom needs me at all now-a-days. Hardly comes to this place after losing our son and his family, especially Susan. Wasn't real sure she would make it this time. But now, hearing about this, I suppose she'll be along directly." His smile widened. "You are the first, you know."

"First?" Brice squinted.

"Yes. Very special thing that is." He pointed the

stem of his pipe at Brice. "The first family, the Mullins I believe, gave up what monies they had invested in this place and walked out on the loan after not much more than a year. It seems the crying sounds upset the children. The Stonewalls lasted a whole three years. But they weren't like old Stonewall Jackson at all. The burning Christmas tree did it for them, especially when they spotted the ghost in the middle of it." Looking back at Brice, he added, "Truthfully, I would not have come if Susan wasn't in so much distress. I've seen your Paranormal Detectives specials. Just thought I'd throw my two cents in with you if you don't mind."

"Mind?" Brice shook his hand again. "We would love your help."

Clarence smiled as he lit his pipe.

"Do you think you can help us, Sir?" asked Heather.

Blowing a perfect circle away from them, he softly replied, "Like you wouldn't believe."

Anna nodded toward Hershey. "Looks like you've made a friend, Mr. Christopher."

"Yes." He knelt down and petted the lab. "He's a very beautiful animal. You must love him very much."

"We do," answered Anna as she looked out the front window. "I don't see your car. Did it leave you?"

"Ohhh, I don't drive much anymore. When I get ready to leave, it will come for me." Looking back to Brice he asked,

"Would you please take me to where you last saw Susan?"

"Anna?" Brice turned to his daughter.

"Hailey and I would be proud to," replied Anna. "I believe she stays in her closet most of the time."

"God bless me," whispered Clarence as he followed

the two girls up the stairway. "That was her 'Safe Place' you know. Whenever she was sad or scared, or disappointed, she would stay in there until whatever storm that was troubling her would blow over."

Anna paused at the open doorway of their bedroom, but the

Labrador went directly to the foot of the beds and sat down between them, staring at the closed, closet door.

"This has been quite an experience for us, sir," explained Hailey. "We've never had this kind of excitement before." She turned and pointed to the closet. "If I had to guess where she was, I would look in the far, right corner first. Hershey usually knows where she's at."

But as the old fellow entered the bedroom, the two girls were distracted by another, loud knock upon the front door.

Clarence paused, looking back at the girls. "I believe that would be my wife, Jackie. Would you two please escort her up here when she is ready? I'm quite sure she will want to come."

"Yes, sir. We would be glad to." Anna and Hailey turned, went down the stairs, and then paused at the foot of the steps.

"That's got to be her," whispered Hailey as Birmingham let the two visitors in. "Well-combed gray hair, patent leather shoes, matching bag, and camel coat. Gosh, she looks older than her husband—nineties at least. I'll bet that red Cadillac is out there right now."

Anna looked toward the front windows. "No Cadillac. Looks like a black Lincoln."

"Look there," whispered Hailey, nodding to a young black man standing just inside the door way. "He must be her driver."

"Yes," whispered Anna." The man was tall and

thin, black jacket and cap with a patent leather bill. "He's certainly dressed the part."

Mrs. Christopher's driver drew close to her left side with his hand tucked inside her upper right arm as Birmingham led them into the living room.

"Mrs. Christopher." Brice stood from the couch as did Heather. "I'm so glad to see you could make it. Won't you have a seat?"

"Uhhh . . ." Distracted by Anna and Hailey at the foot of the stairs, she paused, smiling at the young girls. "So nice to see this old place come alive once more."

"Thank you," replied Heather. "These are our two daughters, Anna and Hailey. My son, Hunter is in his room playing with his erector set. He likes to build things."

"I hope you get to see Susan," replied Hailey. "I'm sure she would be most pleased. I'm so glad the two of you could come."

"Susan?" Mrs. Christopher paused again, almost losing her smile. "Child, did you say two?" She glanced at her driver.

"Now Mrs. Jackie . . ." The driver threw a desperate glance at Birmingham. "You know you don't need to get your blood pressure up again."

"Dear," ignoring the driver, Mrs. Christopher looked back at Hailey. "Were you speaking of my driver, Jonesy? We're the only two at The Hills now."

"Not exactly, Ma'am," Anna glanced at her Father. "Not long before you came in, we had another visitor. When we came downstairs, he was dusting off the old, Hamilton clock there by the fireplace."

"Uhh oh," groaned Jonesy, looking once again at Birmingham.

"Now-now," grumbled Mrs. Christopher. Pushing her driver's hand from her, she looked to Anna. "He never believes me. What did he look like, dear?"

"Ohhh, a little younger than you and about your height, I guess-thin, light-colored hair, gray pants, plaid vest, and the strangest, little glasses."

Mrs. Christopher gripped her driver's arm. "Gold, wire rims with oval lenses?"

"Yes Ma'am. He was fidgeting with his briarwood pipe."

"Ohhh . . ." The old lady swooned as Birmingham rushed up from behind her.

"Take her to the couch," instructed Birmingham, holding tightly to her left arm.

"Her purse!" Jonesy grabbed her purse, rummaged through it, and then produced a glass bottle of little, white pills. "I need a glace of water please."

"Got it." Heather dashed off toward the kitchen.

Mrs. Christopher took a seat on the couch. Her eyes batted wildly as she patted her chest.

"Here, here." Heather produced a glass of water and a damp face cloth.

"Jonesy, Jonesy?" she said, gripping the glass of water.

"A little water and then put the pill under your tongue," directed the driver.

Brice worked a pillow behind her and encouraged her to lean back against it.

"Mrs. Jackie," Jonesy patted her hand, "please don't get your hopes up again." Glancing at the others, he added, "She's been dreamin' of Mr. 'C' all week. Uhhh, that would be Mr. Clarence, her husband. He passed some time ago."

"My-my." Birmingham stepped back, staring at the ceiling. "Jus' when I thought everything was about to smooth out."

"He's here," chimed in Hailey.

"That kind of thing's not doin' her any good!" exclaimed Jonesy, glaring at Hailey.

Mrs. Emily walked from the kitchen, pausing at the living room entranceway. "The young lady's right." She nodded toward the girls. "I saw those two take him right up those stairs not twenty minutes ago. I don't much believe in ghosts, but I do believe in angels. Maybe that's what we have right now."

Mrs. Christopher immediately grabbed Jonesy's arm and pulled herself to a sitting position. "Take me, Jonesy. Take me right now."

"Now, Mrs. Jackie," complained Jonesy, "That's a long, bunch o' steps for you take on right now."

"Right now!" she snapped, trying to stand. "If it kills me, it kills me, but I've at least got to try."

"I got her. I got her." Birmingham rushed to her left side.

Now, with Birmingham on her left side and Jonesy on her right, Mrs. Christopher slowly led the rest up the stairway. "Clarence said that he would see me soon," she said. "I thought my time was drawing near. But here we are, aren't we?"

"My-my," complained Birmingham. "I got the same feelin' the closer we get to that door."

"It's the one on the left," prompted Hailey. "Just follow the bannisters."

Jonesy looked at Birmingham as they reached the top of the stairs. "You all are serious about this Mr. Christopher thing, aren't you?"

"And other things." Birmingham's eyes wide, he stopped the procession half way to the partially closed door. "Ohhh Mr. Elmore!" He nodded toward the bedroom doorway, only a few steps away. "The whole bedroom's lit up and there ain't no light in there that's that bright."

"We'll take her from here," said Hailey, glancing at her sister.

"You two girls lead the way," instructed Mrs. Christopher. "Follow them, she added, now holding tightly to Birmingham

"What?" Birmingham looked to Brice.

"Go on, Mr. B," coached Mrs. Emily from the rear of the group.

Mrs. Christopher tugged at his arm, watching Anna open the door wider.

"The light's coming from the closet," whispered Hailey. "Come on, Birmingham," complained Mrs. Christopher. "Don't falter on me now. I don't want to miss him. He's got to be with Susan." She paused next to Anna and Hailey, just inside the doorway.

"My-my." Birmingham led the little lady from between Anna and Hailey and entered the bedroom. His eyes shifted from the open closet door to Hershey, still at the foot of the beds, nosing his favorite, red ball.

"Hershey. Come here." Anna started forward, but was stopped by her father.

"He'll be fine, dear," said her father. "Let's give Mrs. Christopher a little time. If we crowd in now, we may lose everything."

Those words were no sooner said than the light from the closet began to fade. Seeing that, Hershey jumped up and bounded into the closet.

"Hershey!" Hailey pulled away from her father, ran past Birmingham and Mrs. Christopher, and then stopped, gazing into the dark of the closet. "Hershey! Hershey!" she cried. Tears streamed down her cheeks as she moved the long dresses about for a better look at the floor."

"The light is gone." Mrs. Christopher pulled away from Birmingham and eased up beside Hailey.

"How can this be?" sobbed Hailey. "The light took them all away, didn't it?"

Anna rushed in to join them, but could say nothing as she also stared into the closet.

"Come, girls." Mrs. Christopher nodded toward

Hailey's bed. "Sit with me a while and let me catch my breath."

Mrs. Christopher, somehow, found the strength to support Hailey as the young girl seemed to cry for both of them. But as the grand, old lady sat there consoling her, Birmingham's "Uh oh," caught her attention. He was, as were the others with him, looking at the closet once more.

"Here we go again." Birmingham's voice weak.

"Clarence?" Mrs. Christopher struggled back to her feet, staring at the dim light. "Smell that?"

"Tobacco?" Anna jumped to her feet, rubbing the tears from her eyes also.

"The light is back," noted Hailey, still sitting with her eyes glued to the closet.

"Not just the light, the smell of his pipe is there also." Mrs. Christopher edged one step closer as Hailey slowly stood. "That's black cherry pipe tobacco. He finally lit his pipe." Stroking Hailey's brown hair, she added, "My Susan and your Hershey *are* with him right now. They couldn't be in better hands. Come," she added, slowly walking toward the closet. "I want to smell that old pipe as long as I am able."

Anna strained her eyes into the dim glimmer that now dominated the back of the closet. The closer they got, the stronger the black cherry smelled, and the brighter the glimmer became. But as they were almost at the door, the sound of something plopping over and over on the closet floor stopped them.

"Ohhh, wow," whispered Anna as Hershey's ball bounced out of the closet and rolled past them.

The bark was unmistakable. The big Chocolate Labrador bounded out of the closet as if he was in the back yard. Brushing past them, he grabbed the ball, wheeled, and then started back. But it was too late. Hailey grabbed him and knelt, holding tightly to his collar. Not a word was spoken. All in the room were now looking at the rear of the closet, for the light had now filled it once again. The scene was perfect-a little blond girl walking away through a field of red clover with the same, old gentleman they all had met at the grandfather's clock.

"Clarence!" Mrs. Christopher reached out toward her first love. Holding that position, she was obviously praying that he would at least look back at her.

Amazingly, the old fellow stopped, turned, and then pointed them out to the little girl.

"Susan!" Tears rolled down Mrs. Christopher's cheeks as she watched her granddaughter mouth "Grandmother?" They both waved as the light faded to black once more.

"Ohhh, God help me," sobbed Mrs. Christopher as she started to crumple.

"I got her! I got her!" exclaimed Birmingham. He ran forward and helped the girls get Mrs. Christopher back to the bed.

"I have not a soul left here on earth," she sobbed. "And now, the ones I love the most have left me again." She bowed her face to her hands, weeping bitterly.

"Not so." Anna hugged her across her shoulders. "This was your home, Mrs. Christopher. I know you must have thousands of memories here. You are welcomed here anytime you choose to come."

Mrs. Christopher raised her head in an attempt to look at Anna, but was distracted by Hershey's low key whine. The family pet walked to the closet door, looked inside, and then sat down. The ball rolled from his mouth and onto the floor.

"My, my." Birmingham wiped his wet cheeks. "That's a picture I won't soon forget. He looks disappointed, sad, and lamentin'. Yep, he's just seen

Heaven, been there, and then lost it. I 'spect if I was him, I'd be a little sad too."

"Come, Mrs. Christopher." Heather stepped toward the three on the bed and encouraged the grand old lady to stand.

With one, last look at the closet, Mrs. Christopher walked with the girls from the room. Smiling at Brice as she passed, she asked, "Seen anything like this in your investigations?"

"No, Ma'am," he slowly shook his head. "Not even close."

Brice, Mrs. Emily, Birmingham, Jonesy, and even Hershey followed the four from the room and down the stairs to the living room.

Taking a seat on the couch with Anna and Hailey, Mrs. Christopher's gaze wondered past all in the room. "Clarence was a good man, you know," she finally said. "He loved this old house, that old clock, and all the drafts, creaks, and chimes that came with them. We had such a time picking out the furniture for this place. But when the plans for Rolling Hills were formulated, he didn't get involved with any of that. I did it all myself. I don't think it ever seemed like 'home' to him. After he died, the place seemed so empty I could hardly stand it. About a week or so ago, I believe, I had a dream in which he came to me and stood at the foot of my bed. 'Susan can't find her way,' he said just as plain as I'm talking to you right now." Smiling again, she looked down to the handkerchief in her hands. "I didn't really know what he was talking about until I got your call." She glanced at Brice. "I think I'm closer to those two right here than in any other place I could think of." She then looked straight at Brice and Heather. "Would I be in the way if I took you up on your offer every so often?"

Brice shook his head. "We all would be sad if you

didn't, Mrs. Christopher. Please do, and often."

"Then. . ." Her smile widened. "Do me a favor."

"Anything," prompted Anna.

"Please, call me Mrs. Jackie. I never hear that name enough anymore."

"Done, Mrs. Jackie," obliged Brice.

"My-my," groaned Birmingham.

Knowing full well that when Birmingham made that comment, something was about to happen, everyone looked at the old handyman, and then to the grandfather's clock where he was now staring.

"Ohhh, my word." Mrs. Emily's voice weak. "He's done come here and left that old pipe."

Sure enough, resting upon the top, right front corner of the old time piece sat the old, briarwood pipe-still lit and smoking.

"Please . . ." Mrs. Jackie held out her left hand toward it, "bring it to me. I just want to touch it and feel its warmth."

"Go ahead." Brice nodded to Birmingham.

"My-my," complained Birmingham again, faltering in his steps toward the clock.

"I got it," responded Jonesy. Walking briskly to the old clock, he took the pipe from the top molding, and then paused looking about the room. "Think I just got 'a hang on to that 'Angel' thing, Mrs. Emily. Don't much cotton to ghosts."

"He's not here, Jonesy," laughed Mrs. Jackie. "I'm quite puzzled as to why he left it."

Jonesy returned to the couch and placed it in Mrs. Jackie's hands. "It's still warm and smokin', Ma'am."

Cradling it with both hands, she leaned back deep in the couch, shut her eyes, and then took in the smoke now swirling about her.

"I know it's late," started Mrs. Emily, "but the table is still set. We have sliced ham, bologna, sliced cheese, barbecued beans, tomatoes, lettuce, and plenty of fresh bread and tea."

Heather knelt in front of Mrs. Jackie. "Why don't you and Jonesy take a late supper with us? If you would like to stay, we would love to have you."

"That's very kind of you," she replied without opening her eyes. Then, looking at Heather, she added, "Jonesy never complains or asks for anything, but I'm quite certain that he is hungry. Perhaps, if you could—"

"That will be no problem." Heather patted her hand. "But what about you?"

"I'll just sit here for a while if you don't mind. I'm not very hungry right now."

Mrs. Emily motioned for Jonesy to join them. "Jus' follow his lead," she said, gesturing toward Birmingham. His plate was already full and he was still looking.

"I think I'll take my plate in the living room and keep Mrs. Jackie company." said Birmingham.

"Come," encouraged Hailey, holding out a plate for Jonesy as the others gathered about the table. "Do you like barbecued beans?"

"I certainly do, Ma'am," responded Jonesy, almost bragging.

As Hailey served Jonesy's plate, she noticed that Birmingham had stopped just inside the living room entranceway. He wasn't saying a word.

"Birmingham?" Hailey got no reply. "Birmingham!"

"My-my-my," he said, easing on into the room. Slowly lowering his plate to the coffee table, he knelt at the side of Mrs. Jackie.

"Mrs. Jackie!" Jonesy spun around. Dropping his plate to the table, he rushed to her side. "Mrs. Jackie!" he called out loudly as he briskly rubbed her hands.

"Ohhh no." Heather put her plate back on the

table, and rushed to join the two men at the couch. "Mrs. Christopher! Mrs. Christopher!" she called loudly as the others gathered silently at the entranceway.

"This can't be happening," sobbed Hailey as she ran from the room, crying.

Hunter peeped out from his room, watching Hailey run down the hallway, but he remained reluctant to join them.

Slowly standing, Birmingham backed from the couch. "She looks like she's jus' napping." he all but whispered. "She's gone yawl," he managed, glancing back at the others at the entranceway.

"Nooo, she ain't!" snapped Jonesy, still rubbing her hands. "Mrs. Jackie. Mrs. Jackie," he repeated. His voice soft and low.

Birmingham placed a gentle hand upon Jonesy's left shoulder. "She's with Mr. Clarence, Jonesy."

"No she ain't! No-she-ain't!" With tears streaming down his cheeks, Jonesy brushed Birmingham's hand away. "She's jus' sleepin'. She done it before."

"Where's the pipe?" prompted Birmingham.

Jonesy lowered her hands to her lap, slowly looked all about her, and then sat down on the floor at her feet.

"Did anyone see him take it?" asked Brice.

Not a word came for an answer.

Jonesy looked up at Brice. "He had to be here, Mr. Elmore. I didn't say anything when I took the pipe from off the clock, but when I looked in the bowl, it seemed freshly lit. Some of the tobacco hadn't even caught yet."

"My-my," groaned Birmingham.

"Will you quit," snapped Mrs. Emily. "Every time you say that, somethin' else happens."

"Nope," countered the handyman. "Some-thin's already happened is more like it."

Life's strange, ain't it," added Jonesy as tears tracked their way to his chin. "I didn't believe her about Mr. 'C'. Somehow, she knew he was comin' for her. But just as soon as I thought she was wrong, the old fellow shows up and takes her from us." He looked up at Birmingham as if for an explanation.

Birmingham smiled. "My Mrs. Emily don't say much, but when she do, I listen. She always say, 'Never, ever, forget those you love for they will always be with you.' Don't know how Mr. Clarence did it, and I don't even know who he convinced to let him. I only hope that if I go before Mrs. Emily, I can be jus' as convincin' to them that matters."

M. R. Williamson lives with his wife, Connie in Horn Lake, Mississippi and has been an author for over twenty years. His novels are carried by Powel's Bookstore in Portland, Oregon among others. Now, only writing for Hiraeth Books and WolfSinger Publishing, he spends most of his time with the series 'Horned Jack' and 'The Moleskin Cap' (respectively) by those publishers.

"I love the craft," he says. "A writer must always

write what he loves. As for me, I'll stick with Speculative Fiction.

www.ingramcontent.com/pod-product-compliance
Lightning Source LLC
LaVergne TN
LVHW012033060526
838201LV00061B/4577